Fleeting Glimpse

A Frightening Novella

Victoria M. Patton

Dark Force Press

Dark Force Press

City of Publication: Piedmont, OK

www.darkforcepress.com

Publisher's Note: This is a work of fiction. Names, characters, places, and incidents are a product of the author's imagination. Locales and public names are sometimes used for atmospheric purposes. Any resemblance to actual people, living or dead, or to businesses, companies, events, institutions, or locales is completely coincidental.

Fleeting Glimpse/ Victoria M. Patton - 1st Ed.

Print ISBN 13: 978-1-946934-20-8

EBook ISBN 13: 978-1-946934-21-5

Editor: Judith Bixby Boling

Tony, your title and idea spawned my creativity. Thank you!
Thank you to my fabulous beta readers. You make my books
kickass.

Thank you to my editor, Judith Boling. You put up with all my stupid
commas.

Author's Note

Stalking is a real and scary issue for many women and men. If
someone tells you they think they are being stalked, in any form,
please listen.
If you feel you are being stalked or threatened, tell someone.
Make a report to the police.
Don't try to stop it on your own, and don't think you are crazy.
Report it. Get help.
Listen to that inner voice telling you something isn't right. It could
save your life.

Contents

Chapter One

Monday evening

Using my tools, I turn the deadbolt on the side door. The bag containing the dead animal makes a wet squishy sound as it hits the ground. I can retrieve it on my way out. Moving through the empty garage, there is no need for me to use my penlight. I've been here so many times, I know my way around. "Hmph. It's locked." Usually, she doesn't lock the door to the mudroom. It doesn't take much effort to pick this one.

Her perfume hits me the minute I enter her home. Closing my eyes, I bask in the aroma. Vanilla and a hint of orange fill my nostrils. Soon I'll smell it on her skin. Theo rubs against my leg, purring and head butting me. I pick up him up, smiling. "You're getting a little chubby. I think she's been over feeding you since the last time I saw you."

He purrs, rubbing his cheek against my chin, and pawing at my face.

It's surprising how fond I am of him. Rarely do my feelings get in the way. Letting myself get too close can put me at risk. It's something I can't afford to do. Setting the big cat on the floor, I watch him scamper away. "Don't get attached. She's a victim. One that has gotten too much of your attention already." I can't allow myself to be distracted. Distractions lead to mistakes.

The kitchen is immaculate and everything is in its place. The moonlight through the big glass doors makes it just bright enough to see. Walking down the hallway, I stop at the spare bedroom. Not sure why she even has one. She never has any one over.

The glow of a nightlight brings me to her office. A simple wood desk faces the window. The bird feeder is strategically placed, enabling her to watch while she works. No doubt a reprieve when her creativity fails. I pick up the picture of her mother, and move it to the opposite side of the desk.

Heading back to the kitchen, I pause at the glass door, looking at her back porch. The backdrop of trees makes the perfect view. The light fog forming will give me the perfect cover for tonight.

Theo sits next to his empty bowl, eyeing me as I stand in front of the refrigerator. Reading one of the many scraps of paper covering its surface, before opening the door. Shaking my head, I question if this is a place to store food or a giant note board. Some fruit, a container of cottage cheese, several bottles of water, and two bottles of wine fill the otherwise sparse shelves. Shrugging, I look over at Theo. "Maybe she didn't want it to spoil. What do you think?"

He meows, looking at his empty bowl then back at me.

"Did you eat all the food, or did she not leave you enough?" The pudgy creature spins in circles. "I bet two days seems like a lifetime to you." Grabbing his bag of kibbles from the cabinet, I fill his bowl half-way. "There. I wouldn't want your mom to come home and think you suffered." One last look around to make sure nothing will give my visit away. "I'll see you soon, Theo." I smile, leaving the door unlocked.

I flip on the overhead light as I slip out the side door. I can't help myself. I know her habits. This, the unlocked mudroom door, and the photo will drive her crazy. Locking the doorknob, I pull it shut, then use my tools to re-lock the deadbolt. Picking up the small bad, I chuckle. "I hope you like your surprise, Chandra." Opening the lid of the trash bin, I lay the rotting animal on the top of a trash bag, stuffing the bag that carried it down into the bin. Closing the lid, I make my way to the backyard.

Walking across the grass, I don't have to worry about motion sensors or flood lights. She doesn't have any. No alarm either. I move to the edge of the property line on the far-right side. No fencing makes this too easy.

Waiting at the corner of the house, I use the low-hanging branches of a tree to camouflage myself. Glancing over my shoulder, the residents to my right would have to come out and walk to the edge of their driveway before they would be able to see me. Confident in my hiding spot, I focus on the lane.

The late September air is crisp, and the jacket I'm wearing is almost too light. The light fog makes the air feel damp. I didn't realize the temperature would drop this much today. Swallowing hard, I pinch my lips together. Bouncing on my toes, my stomach flutters at the oncoming headlights. My fingers tingle. I clench my fists and quickly release them, dissipating the pent-up energy. An electric like pulse surges through me as I wait for her arrival. "Hurry," I whisper. My teeth chatter. I feel as if I'm moments away from exploding and sending my body parts flying.

A wide grin stretches across my face as she pulls into her driveway. I need to take cover along the thicket of trees in the back. First, I want to see her face. I need to see her face. My insides vibrate, making my skin itch.

Her neighbor exits his home, drawing my attention towards him. I've seen him speak to her. Although I'm never close enough to hear the conversations, her crossed arms and constant frown during their interactions clearly indicate she doesn't like Mr. William Franks. I squeeze my hands into fists, digging my nails into my palms. He's distracting her. My nostrils flare. "Go home." A low growl rumbles in my throat.

Her focus shifts between her garage and Mr. Franks. I can barely see her wrinkled brow as she looks in my direction. She taps her steering wheel, glancing over her shoulder towards her neighbor.

She looks my way one last time, before pulling into her garage. Her brow draws together as she searches the area where I'm standing. I suck in a breath, retreating, stepping back behind the cover of the brick wall. I don't think she sees me. Cursing under my breath, I lean forward and peek around the edge. I could explain my presence away by making the excuse of going for a late evening stroll. But I would rather not give myself away.

I hiss out a breath, watching the tail end of her car pull into the garage. The door closes as Mr. Franks reaches the edge of her lawn. I bite my bottom lip to hide my snicker as I turn to head towards the backyard.

Chapter Two

Inching up to the entrance of her neighborhood, the sensor reads the sticker on Chandra's windshield. The massive gate lumbers open. A guard waves her through without a glance. Calm washes over her, alleviating the achiness in her chest. More and more, she struggles with leaving the security of her home. She finds her anxiety and fear mounting due to the endless stream of interviews, appearances, and book signings.

You don't have any right to complain, Chandra.

Her late mother's words echo in her head. "I know, Mother." She chastises herself. Exhaling, she blows out the guilt. She lives a great life. Nothing to complain about. When she turned in that first story to her now agent, Jane, Chandra had no idea how much her life would change.

She takes in the neighborhood as she drives to her home. Her writing career took off way faster than she or her publishing company, Baker and Son, thought it would. And although she loves creating stories that everyone reads, she is in a constant battle with how much of her private life she has to give up.

If she had her way, she would rather stay at home, write her books, and never talk to strangers again. Her reclusive, introvert personality gets in the way of her public life. "Too late now to change anything, or leave." Her publishing company owns her life, and her agent would shoot her before she let her walk away.

Driving down her lane, a smile creeps across her face. She shimmies in her seat when her house comes into view. "I'm so glad to be home." On the road for two days, Chandra's excitement bubbles over. At 3,800 square feet, her house is on the smaller side. More like a bungalow than the mini-mansions in this community.

Chandra shakes her head as she passes Mr. Franks. "I bet he's going to water his bushes again." Exhaling a sharp deep breath, she waves at him; giving him a half-smile. "What a pompous ass," she says, rolling her eyes. Tapping the remote control on her visor, she watches the garage door crawl open. Over her shoulder she can see Mr. Franks making his way towards her.

"Let's go." Chandra taps the steering wheel, mentally willing the door to raise faster. Peering out her side window, she returns her attention to the garage. She grips the wheel so tight, the veins in her forearms bulge. Another quick glance to her right, and she can see Mr. Franks is almost at her lawn.

The hair on her arms stand on end. Her gaze is drawn towards the left side of her house. "What is that?" She squints in the direction of the movement. The drooping limbs of the trees and the light fog make it impossible for her to make anything out.

Frowning she turns back to her garage door. She blows out the burning air from her lungs as the door slowly opens. The glaring overhead lights illuminate her usually dark garage. "Why is my light on? I shut it off." She can feel her face tighten as her brow wrinkles.

A second movement at the corner of her house catches her eye. Her grip tightens on the steering wheel. Searching, she finds nothing but swaying branches. She chalks it all up to the wind. "Crap," she says, realizing Mr. Franks is steps away from her driveway. The last thing she wants to hear is his opinion of her latest novel.

She guns her motor, lurching forward. Shaking her fist in triumph, she laughs. "Ha," she squeals in delight. "Not this time, William." Rolling in faster than she needed, the windshield hits the tennis ball hanging from the ceiling a little too hard. The ball swings violently, crashing into the glass, bouncing upward. Before she's even parked, Chandra lowers the garage door.

The victorious moment is short lived. The thudding from the ball echoes in the silent garage. Squinting, she stares at the lights. Her mind races and her breathing is shallow. "I turned those off. I know I did." She thinks back to Saturday when she left, replaying her departure in her head. "I fed Theodore, grabbed my purse, my bags, turned on the garage light, opened the door…." She rubs her forehead. "I'm positive I turned off the light before leaving."

Her heart pounds out a beat in her ears. Her stomach churns as her chest tightens, making it hard to catch her breath. *What if someone got in my house?* She lays her head against the wheel. "Stop, Chandra. No one got into your damn house."

Jumping when her phone blares through the Bluetooth, she clutches her chest. She taps the call button. "Hello?" she says, lifting it from the cradle, shifting the call from the speakers to the handset.

"Chandra, it's Adam."

"Hey, Adam. What can I do for you?"

"Are you okay? You sound weird."

"I'm fine. Just got home and was pulling into my garage. What do you need?" She hears drawers opening and paper shuffling. "Are you at the office?" Picking up her purse and briefcase from the passenger seat, she gets out and retrieves her small suitcase from the back. Before heading into her house, she glances at the side door, making sure she indeed locked it.

"Yes, I'm still at the office. Jane had a late evening meeting with Corey Richards. Her new acquisition. He's in California and wasn't available until tonight. Listen, your book signing, the one here in town on Wednesday, the bookstore owner asked if you could come earlier and do a special meet and greet."

Chandra's shoulders sag as she leans her head back. Squeezing her eyes shut, she waits a minute before responding.

"Chandra? Hello?"

"Yeah, Adam. I'm sure I don't have a choice. That's fine." She sighs. "I'm sorry. I know it isn't your fault, but I thought these things were supposed to be prearranged. It's kind of late notice for a book signing." Balancing the phone between her ear and shoulder, she uses her key to unlock the mudroom door. Realizing the door is unlocked, she grunts. "What the heck?" She steps over the threshold.

"Chandra, what's wrong?"

She sighs in exasperation. Dropping her briefcase on the floor and rolling her suitcase out of the way, Chandra turns the lock on the doorknob. "I don't know, Adam. My door is unlocked." Twisting the lock on the knob, she double checks making sure it's secure before closing the door and locking the deadbolt.

"Did you leave it unlocked?"

"No. I never leave my door unlocked. Or my garage lights on for that matter."

"Uh, okay. Chandra, you're sounding kind of frazzled. What's going on?"

"I don't know. I'm just tired."

"Are you sure?"

"Yes." Chandra pinches her lips together to keep from saying anything. Every time she tries to tell Jane or Adam about the weird things happening, they blow her off, telling her it's just her imagination, or her shyness.

She knows her shyness is an issue. But she knows the difference between being uncomfortable around people and the sensation of being watched, or the feeling someone has been in her home. But she also doesn't want to sound crazy. Not a good look for a bestselling author whose publishing house is planning a big tour.

Bringing her to the other reason she keeps her mouth shut. She doesn't want to be seen as trying to get out her upcoming book tour. She's been paid a handsome fee for her books. Chandra knew there would be things she had to do in return. "It's nothing. What do you need?" Carrying her purse into the kitchen, she places it on the table. Slipping out of her shoes, she grabs a bottle of wine from the fridge.

"Meooow!"

"Aww, hi, sweetie." Holding her phone in her hand, she sets the bottle on the counter, and scoops up Theodore, a long-haired Norwegian mix. She grunts as she lifts him, staring at the long whiskers on his face. "Theo, they say a cat's whiskers grow in proportion to the width of the cat. How long do you think yours are going to grow, huh?"

Theodore narrows his eyes at her, scowling.

She sniffs his fur. "You smell good. You've been into something." Giggling at his expression, she checks the large bowl of dry food she left out. "I see you didn't eat it all. I guess you didn't starve to death."

"Uh, excuse me?"

Laughing at Adam's response, she grabs a can of cat food from the cupboard. "I was talking to my cat."

Theodore wiggles in excitement, trying to leap from her grasp.

"Okay, calm down. Adam, give me a few minutes."

"Sure," he says.

She sets the phone on the counter.

Theo jumps from her arms spinning in circles waiting for his food.

Grabbing a dish from the cabinet, she empties the contents of the can. She holds her breath for a few seconds. "Wow! How can you eat this stuff?" she asks, setting it down.

Theo purrs as he gobbles his food.

"Slow down, Theodore," she says, picking up the phone. "Okay, Adam, sorry about making you wait. Why wasn't this meet and greet prearranged?"

"Thomas arranged it. However, after Jane fired him, he still had access to his editor log in and remotely deleted vital information and several of your appointments. Had it not been for the shop owner calling us, you would have missed it."

"Oh darn," Chandra says, concentrating on balancing the phone and a bottle of wine, as she pulls a wine glass from its hanging perch. The clink of glass gives her pause. Cringing, she watches the stemware sway.

"These aren't bad, Chandra. They're more intimate, and your fans love them."

"That may be true, but…" Chandra shakes her head. "Has there been any other fallout from Thomas?" She grabs a bottle opener from a drawer.

Adam sighs into the phone. "Yeah. He's going to sue you and Jane."

"Me? Why me?" Her voice stammers.

"He says you got him terminated, and Jane hasn't paid him his last salary check."

"How did I get him fired? He tried to trick me into signing with another publisher, all under the guise of Jane's approval. He got himself fired."

"You don't have anything to worry about. He can't touch you. Or us, for that matter."

"That's what you say. When is this shindig?" Frowning, she pinches her lips together to keep from saying anything snarky. Pouring some wine into her glass, she takes a long sip. It's the first time she relaxes since she returned home.

"Hang on, I have the information somewhere," Adam pauses. "Here it is. Five p.m. With the main book signing starting at seven."

"All right. Can you make sure to bring me a few hard cover books?"

"I can do that."

"Thank you." Her voice trails off. She's standing in front of her automatic sliding glass doors, peering at her backyard. She loves the unfiltered view these doors give. Their seamless construction and interlocking panes mean no clunky doors on a track. The original doors were like that, and the owner had a huge metal dowel attached for security. These doors provide the security she wants without the bulky ugly frame.

Chandra loves her backyard view. It's why she purchased the home. The odd shape of her property gives her lots of privacy from her neighbors who are over a hundred feet away on either side. Due to the curvature of the cul-de-sac, her house sits at the front of the lot, giving her a smaller front yard. While roughly one and a half acres sits at the back. The property lines give her backyard the shape of an inverted triangle, placing her home at the tip.

The half-moon mesmerizes Chandra as Adam's voice drones on about the bookstore. Its subtle glow, combined with the light fog, casts soft shadows against the backdrop of the dense row of evergreens encircling her entire property. The trees whisper for her to join them.

Adam continues to go over her upcoming schedule. A month-long tour of the northeast, beginning with her home town of Manchester, New Hampshire, traveling the coastline, with several stops at bookstores along the way. Chandra's chest tightens. She doesn't want to be gone that long. The only saving grace, she gets to take Theodore with her.

If she has to discuss business, she might as well be comfortable. Wrapping herself up in a blanket from the back of a reading chair, she prepares to go out on the deck. Using the ball of her foot, she presses the locking mechanism that will allow for the glass doors to slide open.

Chapter Three

The solid line of trees separating the properties from each other gives me the perfect hiding spot. The fog encircles each solar light on the steps from the wooden deck, creating a muted glow. A burning sensation fills my chest. I can see her on the phone as she grabs the wine from the fridge. "Get off the phone." A growl vibrates at the back of my throat. "And come outside." Clenching my jaw, the corded braids of tension seize in my neck.

I step out and move a little closer. She's standing at the large sliding glass doors. Wiping my moist palms on my jeans, my tongue slides across my lips. My heart skips a beat as I inch closer, leaving the seclu-sion of the trees. I want to be near her. I want to smell her perfume and touch her cheek, feel her skin under my fingertips.

"Come outside, Chandra." The softness of my voice floats on the cold air around me. Taking another step closer, I hug the tree line. I'm sure she can't see me. I'm nearing a jut out of trees. To keep her in view, I need to step out onto the open grassy area. Hugging the branch-es as best I can, I maneuver around them, moving closer to my prize.

It's the perfect night. I've let this go on long enough. The pounding of my pulse quickens, beating out a rhythm in my chest. She's right there, so close. If she would just step out onto the porch, I can take her. I plead silently, begging her to come outside. Saliva coats my mouth, and my breathing is raspy as trembling takes over my body.

Chapter Four

"I think the timing of this book tour and the publication of your latest book works great for fall. Especially with Halloween just around the corner," Adam says.

"Mmhm," is the only response Chandra can muster. The wine coats her throat and soothes the pangs of anxiety trying to creep up her spine. Adjusting the blanket, she reaches for the sliding door remote sitting on a little table near her. Her fingers graze it before she yanks her hand back. The hair on her neck bristles. Her stomach drops as her pulse thrashes in her ears.

"What did you say, Chandra?"

"Nothing. Keep going. You mentioned a Halloween party?"

"Yes, it's at A Page Turner book store. One of the stops on your tour. The owner has set up a haunted forest on his property."

Moving towards the wall, Chandra flicks off the interior lights. Squinting she tries to see through the fog to the edge of the trees. She's having a hard time making out the details, but she's positive she saw something or someone. Stepping up to the glass door, she scans her backyard. Even though she doesn't see anything, she decides her back porch may not be such a good idea. She turns towards the kitchen when something along the far-right corner catches her attention. In a thicket of trees, there's a silhouette. She gasps as she steps back.

"Chandra? Are you okay? What's going on?"

Her eyes bulge, and the instant dryness keeps her from blinking. Chandra's entire body is engulfed in tremors. Her shallow breaths burn her throat. Her shaking hand makes the wine slosh around.

"Chandra? Hello? What's going on?"

Adam's high pitch voice and barrage of questions bring her out of the trance. "I think I saw someone in my backyard."

"Really? Where? Are they still there?"

"No. Not now." Chandra blows out a shaky breath, moving further away from the window. Remembering the lock, she steps to the right, near the edge of the door. Using her foot, she presses the locking mechanism. Eliminating the possibility of the glass partitions being pried open.

"Maybe it's the shadows playing tricks on you."

She cringes at his response. "Yeah, it probably is," she says taking two big gulps of wine.

"Isn't your neighborhood gated?"

"Yes, it is."

"You could always call the guards at the gate. Have them come and check for you."

"I could do that." Chandra putters around the kitchen. Not wanting to be on the phone any longer.

"What's the matter?" Adam asks.

"Nothing."

"Tell me." Adam prods.

"They will just think I'm crazy. That's all."

"Call them anyway if it will give you peace of mind."

"Maybe I will."

"Chandra, you're worrying me."

"How am I worrying you? What am I doing?"

"You've mentioned you think you've seen the same man at a few of your book signings. I also know you don't like being front and center. But you're the face of Baker and Son right now. There are some things you have to do. The publishing company is paying you pretty good money. I don't think I have to tell you what they expect of you."

Chandra's nostrils flare. "I know what they expect of me. That's for damn sure. Doesn't mean I have to like it."

"No. You don't. But sometimes I think you let your anxiety and worry get the best of you. Couple that with you not liking the focal point, it just seems like you make it harder than it has to be."

Chandra's head hangs low. She should never have mentioned the fan to Adam. She doesn't know what she thought she would get by reaching out to him for help. "Okay. Is there anything else?"

Adam sighs into the phone. "Nothing really. It can wait until our meeting next week. Chandra, try not to worry. Most fans really are harmless. With that said, knowing you, I think you should alert your security. Please don't revert to the shy Chandra."

Sighing, she swallows the last few sips of her wine. "I won't. I'll call security. If nothing else, I'm going to bed. Goodnight, Adam."

"Goodnight."

Placing the glass in the sink, Chandra scans the backyard, through the kitchen window. Nothing seems out of place. No more shadows. No more boogeymen. She closes the small curtain anyway. Wanting to get rid of that creepy feeling, she closes the drapes on all the first-floor windows.

She uses the remote for the sliding glass door to engage the smart glass. When she had this door installed, she made sure it had the ability to frost the glass for privacy. She liked being able to keep outsiders from looking in, but letting the sun shine through during the day.

Theodore weaves in and out of her legs, pawing at them every few turns. "Are you ready for bed?" Picking him up, she snuggles him tight against her chest. Reaching the stairs, she stops. She looks at the security phone on the wall. Taking a step towards it, she reconsiders. Turning back to the stairs, she sighs. Her shoulders droop as she picks up the phone.

"Security."

"Hey, this is Chandra Willis, at 1425 N. Alabaster."

"Yes, Ms. Willis. What can I do for you?"

"You're going to think I'm crazy. I'm not, I promise."

"We get all kinds of calls. What's going on?" the guard asks.

"When I came home tonight, I found my garage light on and one of my doors unlocked."

"Did you leave the light on or the door unlocked?"

A slight snicker fills Chandra's ear. "No. I didn't. I never do. Then, a few minutes ago, I thought I saw someone at the edge of my back yard. Lurking in the evergreens. Listen, could you send someone to give a quick check?"

The security guard pauses.

"Hello?"

"Sorry, Ms. Willis. We'll be by in a few minutes."

"Okay. I'll wait to speak with you." Hanging up the handset on the wall, Chandra heads to the sofa. Theodore curls up on her lap. Scratching his head, her eyes slowly drift shut.

Chapter Five

"Closing all the drapes and frosting the glass won't keep me away, Chandra. It just means I have to wait. And being patient is something I'm very good at." Walking back to my car, I laugh. Security gates. What a joke. They are manned by men who are paid a few more dollars than minimum wage and don't really care about the safety of those in their fold.

Parked across from the construction area, my truck blends in well with those of the other workers. No one ever questions it being parked here. "Why would they? They could care less." Pulling out of the temporary parking area, I turn towards my home. "I think it's time to get a little closer to you, my beloved."

Chapter Six

BANG!

Sitting up, she clutches her fist to her chest as her breath pants in and out. Chandra shakes her head, trying to clear the haze.

Theodore jumps off her lap, hissing.

"What the hell?" Her eyes dart around the room. The clock on the wall says twenty minutes have passed since she called security.

Her legs wobble under her weight. The tingling in her chest morphs into a painful sharpness, making it hard for her to take a deep breath. Creeping towards the glass door, she uses the remote to clear the opaque frost.

A dark blob rests about three feet from her. She can't make it out. As she steps closer, a knock on the front door rattles her. She blows out a shaky breath, glancing over her shoulder towards the knocking. She turns her attention to the back deck, venturing closer to the door.

Chandra frowns. She reaches for the deck lights when another round of knocking makes her rethink her boldness. Just as she turns towards her front door, she hears footsteps on the deck. Chandra spins around. She screams, running from the man standing on the other side of the glass.

"Ms. Willis? Are you okay?" The knocking intensifies. "Ms. Willis?"

Yanking open the door, she points to her deck. "Someone is out there," Chandra says, looking over her shoulder before turning back to the security guard.

The man peers around her. "I don't see anyone."

Lowering her head, she glares at the security guard. "I saw someone on my back porch." Her brow draws together. She opens her mouth to say something, then closes it. She looks at her glass door. "I swear, a man was standing on my deck."

George angles his head to the side. He stares at Chandra with one eyebrow raised. "I think you might have seen my partner, Jeffrey."

"Oh," she says, as instant relief washes over her. "That's good to know." She can see the amusement in George's expression. "Right before you knocked on my door, I heard a loud bang. Like something hit the glass doors. I guess it startled me."

"I'm sorry. I sent him around the back while I knocked on the door. I didn't mean for him to scare you."

Nodding, she gives him a half smile. "That's all right. I think there is a dead animal on my porch." Her voice trails off. She wonders just how crazy she sounds.

"You mean this?" Jeffrey says, walking up next to George.

"What is it?" She leans back as he holds the dead creature in front of her.

"Looks like a bird may have dropped his prey. A rat or something."

Chandra cringes back from Jeffrey and the giant headless rat-like creature dangling from his hand. A few blood drops splatter at his feet. "Oh, my gosh. That's gross."

Jeffrey smiles. "I'm guessing a bird got spooked and dropped his dinner."

George smirked at his partner, who moved to stand closer to him. "I bet this is the sound you heard before we showed up," he points to the dead animal.

She squints at the two men, no doubt enjoying themselves at her expense. "Did you find anyone on the property?"

Jeffrey shook his head. "No, ma'am. I couldn't see any evidence of an intruder. It's pretty hard to get into this neighborhood, although it's not impossible. Even though the construction entrance is manned by security, someone could still get in."

"That doesn't make me feel secure," Chandra says.

George elbows his partner. "Ignore him. There wasn't any sign of an intruder."

Nodding, she steps back, breaking eye contact as she begins to close the front door. "Thank you for checking. I'm sorry I bothered you."

"You're welcome, and you're no bother, Ms. Willis," George says.

"We'll dispose of this for you." Jeffrey lifts the dead animal.

Chandra grimaces. "Thank you. I hate for it to sit in my bin until trash day."

"Call us if you have any other problems, Ms. Willis."

Watching as they get into their souped-up golf cart, she shudders at the sound of her deathly quiet home. Turning around, Theodore is waiting for her.

She quickly turns the sliding glass doors opaque before scooping up the cat. "Enough spooky excitement for one night. Let's go to bed." She scoops up the cat, heads upstairs, and locks her bedroom door behind her.

Chapter Seven

Tuesday morning

A loud sound echoes through Chandra's head like a jackhammer. "No. I don't want to get up." Fumbling for the snooze button on the alarm clock, she hits it several times before it shuts off. Rolling over, clutching her pillow, the warmth from the cover lures her back to sleep. The smell of honeysuckle and fresh-cut grass fills her senses. She can feel the soft grass as it squishes between her toes. A light warm breeze blows over the open field.

Bzzz. Bzzz. Bzzz.

The soft fabric of her pillowcase helps block out the annoying bee buzzing around her head. "Go away." Slowly the buzzing grows louder. Blinking, Chandra takes a chance, looking out from the protection of her coverings. Glaring red numbers fill her blurry vision. "Shit!"

Chandra pops out of her daze, leaping from her bed. "No, no, no. I can't believe how much I overslept." No time to ease into her day, she runs to her bathroom, turning on the shower. "This is going to cut it close." The warmth of the water makes her feel as if she could melt into a puddle. *I wonder how much trouble I would be in if I skipped it.* "Jane would shoot you. That's how much trouble you would be in." She lifts her face letting the water cascade over her.

In seven minutes, her hair is washed and conditioned. Barely dry, the towel goes on her head. Naked in front of the mirror, she preps her face with moisturizer. Ogling her boobs, she wonders how much more they're going to sag before she hits forty. Gone are the days of her once perky assets. "I can't remember the last time I let someone see me with nothing on," she mumbles. "Too long, that's for sure."

After applying eye shadow, mascara, and lip color, Chandra checks her face. "At least I won't scare little kids." Twisting her head from side to side she inspects her work. "Thank goodness this is a radio interview." She tosses the towel from her head onto the floor as she darts into her closet.

Standing in front of her clothes, she scans her blouses. Organized by color and grouped by sleeve length, her nose crinkles. "I have no idea what the weather will be. Chilly. I'll go with that." Turning to the other side of the closet, she searches for something warmer.

Ten minutes later, dressed in jeans, boots, and her favorite pink sweater, she walks back into the bathroom. Shaking out her curly hair, the shoulder length bob hangs limp. "Ugh, I can't go looking like a wet rat." Opting for an updo, she pulls down a few tendrils of curls to frame her face.

Theodore is hot on her heels as she runs down the stairs. "Meow, meooow!"

"Yes, I'll feed you. Quit trying to trip me."

His bowl of dry food is half full. There is one last can of wet food on the shelf. "Here, fatty." She scratches his head before walking out the door with her purse. Her breath hitches as she unlocks the mudroom door entering the garage. This time she makes sure the light is turned off and the door is locked, as she hits the garage door opener on the wall. Chilly air rushes at her. Shivering, Chandra is grateful she chose a sweater.

The early morning sun offers brightness but no warmth. She cranks the heater as she backs out. Chandra pauses at the end of her driveway, making sure the door closes. Keeping her speed in check, she drives as fast as she can to the gate. Her left foot taps the floorboard. "Let's go already."

The dash clock says she has less than forty minutes to get to the other side of the city. Chandra winces. With traffic, she'll be lucky to be there with ten minutes to spare. "Crap, let's go." She glares at the gate.

As it swings outward, Chandra inches forward, driving out onto the main boulevard before the gate is fully open. "Finally." Driving a little too fast, she makes her way through the suburbs and hits the freeway, heading to downtown Manchester.

Chapter Eight

Armed with a hot coffee, I'm waiting at an outside café, a half a block down from the radio station. The steam from my cup swirls upward through the chilly air, spinning like a ballerina dancer. All week the radio advertised today's big interview with horror author Chandra Willis. Because of that, there are quite a few gathered outside the station entrance.

Connecting my Bluetooth earpiece to my phone, I pull up the station on the Internet. Lifting my gaze, I have a clear view of the street. The weight of my legs rest on the balls of my feet as they bounce up and down.

I check and recheck my watch. "Chandra, I can't believe you would keep me waiting." I clench my teeth, causing a dull ache at the base of my jaw line.

"Can I get you a snack?"

I shake my head at the annoying waitress who keeps checking on me. "No," I say, lifting my coffee cup. "This is all I need."

"Okay. Well, let me know if I can get you something." She smiles, winking at me.

I angle my head down and follow her with my gaze. She's a pretty girl, but not my type. Chuckling to myself, I'm not sure what my type is. Sitting up straight, I adjust my jacket as Chandra's vehicle pulls into a parking spot almost directly in front of the radio station.

A tingling ache fills my chest, and spreads throughout my body. "Oh, Chandra. You look perfect," I whisper, clasping my hands together in a death grip to keep from waving at her. Watching her exit her vehicle, she glances in my direction. I can see her smile, moments before she is surrounded by her fans.

Her pink sweater hugs her curvy figure, and my mouth waters at her voluptuousness. My pants tighten around me. The thick fabric contains my arousal, doubling the throbbing sensation. I watch as she signs a few books and rushes through the crowd into the station. A sneer creeps across my face. *I can't leave without saying hello.*

Chapter Nine

"Oh no," Chandra gasps as she drives down the street leading to the station. A small crowd of fans are waiting for her arrival. Her hands are sweaty. She wipes them on her jeans. Blowing out a deep breath as she parks in front of the station, she smiles at the small swarm of fans.

"Chandra Willis, will you sign this?"

A young man shoves his book in front of her. She's unprepared and scrambles looking through her purse for a pen. "Here you go."

Another fan sticks their book in her face, then another. Several clamor for selfies and hug her. She pushes through the crowd opening the door to the station.

The young receptionist rushes over to her. "I'm Cathy. I'm so sorry. They weren't here fifteen minutes ago. We had no idea anyone would show up at the station." She helps Chandra in, then locks the doors.

"Neither did I," Chandra says, letting out a nervous laugh.

"We'll make sure you have a security escort to your car." Cathy gives her a shallow smile. "I'm really sorry. We had no idea this would happen."

"It's okay. Hopefully they'll be gone by the time I'm done." Chandra breathes out a long breath.

"Oh, Ms. Willis, I know you probably don't want to hear this now," she says, pushing a button under her desk. "I'm such a big fan." She leads Chandra through the doorway. She leans into the author. "I've read all your books."

"Thank you."

"I just bought your latest one." She stops, placing her hand on Chandra's forearm. "Can I just say, I read through chapter ten and had to get up and turn on all the lights."

Laughing, Chandra reaches into her purse and pulls out a business card. "Email me, and I'll send you a signed copy."

Her eyes widen as she squeals. "Oooh! Seriously? Thank you." Cathy does a little dance in the hallway. "This is so cool. Thank you."

"You're welcome."

The conference room door opens. "Chandra." Roger Pearson smiles.

"Roger, I hope I haven't kept you waiting," Chandra says.

"Not at all. We're having a meeting." He glances at his watch. "You're early as a matter of fact."

"Mr. Pearson," the receptionist says.

"Yes, Cathy?"

"There were a few fans at the station doors. Can we make sure Mrs. Willis has an escort out?"

He looks at Chandra then Cathy. "Why didn't you tell me?"

"I just told Chandra there wasn't anyone there roughly twenty minutes before she showed up. No one told me to have someone posted there. I had no idea they would swamp her at the door."

"Chandra, I'm sorry. We should've prepared better," Roger says.

"It's okay. No one on my team thought there would be anyone here, either. It's really okay."

"Thanks for telling me, Cathy." He motions to others in the conference room. "This is Chandra Willis."

Two men and one woman stand and move around the table to shake her hand.

"Nice to meet you all," Chandra says.

After the introductions, Roger leads the way to the studio. "This is where we will do the radio show. I'm just going to ask a few questions about your books. How you got started and let you give the audience an update on where you plan to be over the next few weeks."

"Sounds like a plan." Chandra stuffs her clammy hands into the pockets of her jeans. Sweat is beading along her hairline. She forces herself to breathe slowly, trying to contain the quiver in her voice.

"Are you sure you're okay? I'm truly sorry about your fans." Roger smiles at her as she sits in the seat at the table in front of one of the microphones.

She nods. "I am."

"Okay then. Let's do this."

• • • ● • ● • ● • • •

At the end of the interview, Roger gives Chandra thumbs up to remove her headset. "You did great," he says, walking towards her. "Was it as bad as you thought it would be?"

"No, not at all. You made me feel at ease." She wiggles a finger at him. "Don't ask me to do it again, though."

"I'm surprised you don't like the spotlight, Chandra. Most authors love getting in front of their fans."

"I love to talk to my fans." She waves her hand over the desk and microphones. "These large-scale interviews, they make me way too nervous." Following Roger out to the lobby, she's greeted by a large vase of roses sitting on the front desk. Two dozen white, with one lone pink one in the center. It's the exact shade of pink as her sweater. "Those are beautiful," she says, smiling at the receptionist.

"They are," Cathy says.

"Your boyfriend has great taste," Chandra sniffs the pink rose.

"Oh, no, they aren't for me." She winks. "They're for you."

Stepping back, Chandra touches the base of her neck. "For me? I...I don't understand."

The young girl shrugs. "They were delivered while you were doing your interview." She points at the bouquet. "There's a card. I bet they're from one of those fans out front earlier."

Chandra's mouth pulls into a tight smile. All eyes are on her, waiting for her to read the card. A slight wave of nausea crests over her. "Either that or my publisher ordered them."

Roger peers out the entrance. "It seems your fans are gone, but I'll walk you to your vehicle just in case."

"I appreciate that. I'm right in front of the station." Lifting the bouquet, she smiles at everyone. "Have a great day," she says walking out.

Roger takes the bouquet from her as she unlocks her door. "These are very pretty." He places them on the floor of the back seat.

"They are. I can't imagine a fan spending money like that on me," Chandra says.

"You'd be surprised what fans will do these days." He closes the car door. "I hope I get to interview you again, Ms. Willis. I have a feeling after this book tour, we will have to bring you in through the back due to the mobs of fans that will show up."

"I don't know about that, but thank you again." Chandra locks her door, retreating in the safety of her car.

Chapter Ten

Driving away from the curb, she pulls the clip out of her hair, shaking her head. She runs her fingers through the loose curls, sighing as the headache trying to take hold subsides. She's about fifteen minutes from home when her agent's ringtone blares through her speakers. "Hello, Jane."

"You were fantastic. We sat here listening to the whole thing."

"It was a simple interview. Nothing special."

"Not according to Roger. He said you were mobbed by some fans?"

"I wouldn't say mobbed, but there were more than I thought would be there. Heck, I didn't think anyone would be there."

"I guess I should've thought about that. After the sales report of your latest book, I should've realized fans might be showing up more and more to your events. Anyway, social media is buzzing about it. Your fans are clamoring for an AMA. We may have to arrange one with call-ins."

Chandra shakes her head. "What's an AMA?"

"Ask me anything."

"No. I don't want to answer questions."

"Why? They love you. You can see that."

"With the tour coming up, I can do Q and A's at the book signings. That's enough." Her head is spinning as she thinks of excuses to get out of doing another radio interview.

"You're going to have to get over your shyness. I don't understand why you have such a hard time with public appearances. I understand today might have been a little bit off-putting, but to be honest, Chandra, this is something you're going to have to get used to. Better sooner than later. Hang on a minute." Jane's muffled conversation filters over the Bluetooth. "Okay, I'm back. Where were we?"

"You were saying I didn't have to do another radio interview."

"Ha, good try. All right, if I can get to the signing tomorrow, I'll be there. Don't hold your breath though. Adam will be there, and he has a preliminary itinerary for you to go over. Your tour will start in two weeks."

Chandra's shoulders droop as the weight of the impending tour hits her. "Oh, fun."

"Stop it. We have you staying at pet-friendly places. Theodore will be well-taken care of. Talk to you later."

"Oh wait, thanks for the flowers."

"What flowers?" Jane asks.

"The bouquet you had delivered to the radio station."

"I didn't have any flowers delivered to the station."

"If you didn't, who did?" Chandra's fingers wrap around the steering wheel. Her knuckles turn white. Her stalker pops into her head.

"I'm not sure, maybe a fan. Maybe Adam. He mentioned he thought you would be nervous about doing this interview. He's way more thoughtful than me."

She forces herself to breathe. "Okay. I'll call him as soon as I get home."

"Hopefully, I'll see you tomorrow night."

The line goes dead. Silence fills the vehicle just as she pulls through the gates of her neighborhood. Parking in her garage, she walks to the mailbox. Returning, she stops midway, and looks over her shoulder. Her body shivers slightly. Glancing around, she sees no one. "It's probably Mr. Franks just waiting to pounce on me." She looks at his windows, seeing if there is any movement as she walks back into the garage. She closes the door before lifting out her flowers.

Theodore stands at the ready, scowl and all, as she enters her home.

"I'm gone for a few hours and this is what I get? Quit glaring at me."

He huffs and turns his butt towards her, prancing away.

Placing the mail, flowers, and her purse on the counter, she returns to the mudroom to grab a box of canned food from the pantry. Filling the big fat kitty's cupboard, she's his new best friend as he rubs his face against her knee. "Now you love me, huh?" She lifts him just enough to give his head a kiss.

"It's dark in here," she says glancing around the house. The only sunshine entering her home is coming from the opaque sliding glass door. Sighing she remembers she didn't have time to open the blinds this morning. She quickly pulls back the heavy drapes from the windows. The shear drapes obscure the view from the outside, giving her a sense of privacy, still letting light through.

"It may be a false sense, but I can't live in a dark home," she says as she uses the remote to make the glass door clear, letting full sun into her home. She grabs her mail and flowers from the counter and carries them to the table. Setting the bouquet in the center, she sniffs the pink flower one more time before opening the small card tucked between the leaves.

Your interview was fantastic.

An uncomfortable quiver settles low in her stomach. "Stop, Chandra. You're making more out of this than you should." She grabs her phone from her purse, dialing Adam's number.

"Hey, Chandra. Congrats on the great interview today."

"Thanks. I hate those things. Your surprise helped. Truth be told, they made my day."

"What surprise?"

"What do you mean—what surprise—the flowers, silly. How did you know pink is my favorite color, and roses are my favorite flower?" Silence fills her ear. "Hello, Adam?"

"I'm confused, what flowers?"

"Huh?"

"What flowers? Chandra, I have no idea what you're talking about. I didn't send you any flowers."

"I came out of my radio interview, and the receptionist handed me a bouquet. I assumed they were from Jane. But Jane said she didn't send them and thought maybe you did." She pants out several sharp breaths.

"No, sweetie, I didn't send them. You need to take a deep breath. I can hear the crazy in your voice."

The hair on the back of her neck bristles. She falls into a chair at the kitchen table. Thoughts of escape race through her head.

"Chandra? Are you still there?"

"Yes—yes, I'm still here."

"Listen, it was probably just a fan. Jane mentioned a crowd showed up at the station. She didn't mention the flowers, though."

"Fans don't usually send flowers. Stalkers do."

"Chandra, you don't have a stalker."

"What about the guy I have seen at a few signings over the last few months?"

"I think he's a fan, nothing more." Adam sighs on the other end. "I know you think the guy from your signings is out to kill you, but I bet, he's just a regular fan. Couple that with you thinking you saw someone in your backyard, I'm sure your anxiety is on overload. You need to get a grip though."

Chandra doesn't say anything.

"I know that sounds dickish, but you have to start getting used to being the center of attention. It's going to come with the territory."

"What do you mean?"

"Unless you quit writing books, you're going to have fans. Some crazy ones, too."

"That's one thing I can do."

"What? Stop writing?" Adam barks out a laugh. "You have three more books to write, you can't go anywhere."

Chandra bites the inside of her lip. The weight of being trapped is pushing down on her. It's a position she doesn't like to be in. Maybe she could give back the advance and walk away.

"Anyway," Adam went on. "I don't think the guy you thought you saw in your backyard is the same as the guy who sent the flowers. I think someone from your neighborhood decided to take an evening stroll. I mean, did the security find anything?"

"No. Just some kind of dead animal a bird dropped."

"Don't you think they would have found something?" Adam asks.

The flowers aren't as pretty now. She frowns at the bouquet. "I guess. Are you going to be at the meet and greet tomorrow?"

"Yes. I'll meet you at the book store at four thirty. We can get the books set up before the private party. Several boxes were delivered to the store. Not sure how many the owner expects to show up. From what I gather, he has invited some prominent people from the community."

The tension between her shoulders spreads out like octopus tentacles, covering her from the top of her head down her back. Chandra arches, twisting from side to side. "Great. I can't wait."

"Don't worry. Okay?"

"Jane said you had an itinerary to go over?"

"I'm not sure I will have it done in time for tomorrow. Chandra, just enjoy the flowers. They're your favorite. Enjoy their beauty."

"All right. I guess so. I have some writing I have to do. I'll see you tomorrow at four-thirty," she says, disconnecting the call.

"Meow,"

"Hey, sweetie." Lifting Theodore, he snuggles against her chin. "What would I do without you? Hmm?" She kisses his pink nose. He rubs his face against hers, his purr sounding like an old jalopy motor. "I think I need to throw these flowers out. I don't want them."

Kissing Theo one more time, she picks up the vase and walks out through the garage to the trash cans. Lifting the lid, she gags. "Oh my gosh, what the hell stinks?" Peeking into the can, right there on the top, is a dead animal. "I thought security disposed of this for me? Hell, I could've thrown it in my garbage can."

Walking back into the garage she bolts the side door along with the mudroom door. She places the flowers back on the table, she stares at them. "They are pretty. I guess I could enjoy them at least for a bit." Chandra lifts the security phone hanging on the wall.

"Security."

"Hey, this is Chandra Willis."

"Oh, hey Ms. Willis, this is George from the other night. Are you okay?"

"I am. I wanted to know why you guys put the dead animal in my garbage can? The one you took from my house. I thought you were going to dispose of it for me?"

"I have no idea what you're talking about. We didn't put any animal in your garbage. We have a special bin for those kinds of disposals. It's emptied more often than trash day."

"You didn't put it in my trash?"

"No, ma'am."

"Well, who put a dead animal in my trash?"

"Do you think one of your neighbors did it, Ms. Willis?"

Chandra presses the palm of her hand against her temple. A ball of molten lava forms in the pit of her stomach. "I don't know. I just don't know."

"Ms. Willis, maybe you should consider getting a security system installed. I have a few I can recommend to you."

A bead of sweat runs down her back as her skin tingles with warmth. "Yeah. Maybe."

"I'll get you a list. Call us if you need anything, Ms. Willis."

"Thank you." Hanging up the phone, Chandra grabs a bottle of water from the refrigerator and a few aspirins from the shelf next to the fridge. Her appetite gone, she scoops up Theo from his perch on the kitchen table, heading towards the living room.

She snuggles into the big soft cushions of her couch, wrapping up in the blanket resting across the back. Curling up on her side, she hugs her cat. "Just a small nap, Theodore. Maybe when we wake up, my headache will be gone."

Her mind races. She thinks about each of her neighbors trying to figure out which one would put a dead animal in her trash bin and why. She keeps to herself. She doesn't bother anyone. "It doesn't matter, anyway. I couldn't prove who did it, even if I knew for sure," she says scratching Theo's head. "Why can't you be a dog? Hmm?"

Theodore is sound asleep next to her. Curled up under the blanket, oblivious to her plight. Within a few moments, her eyes drift shut

Chapter Eleven

The late afternoon sun filters through her windows, casting a warm amber glow throughout the downstairs. Chandra blinks her eyes several times as her vision adjusts to the light. Yawning, she sits up, squinting at the clock on the mantle. "Theo, we slept way too long."

Stretching, she wipes the sleep from the corner of her eyes, heading towards the kitchen. Standing in front of her fridge, she scans the sparsely filled shelves. She looks over at Theo, who sits at his empty bowl. "Well, at least you have food in this house," she says, filling it with dry kibbles.

Opening the door to her pantry, she frowns. Lifting a few things, she inspects the expiration dates. "I should've stopped for groceries on my way home today," she says, shaking her head. "I don't want to get out." She uses the traffic as the reason. But truth be told, she doesn't want to see anyone. Doesn't want to sign a book or pose for a picture.

Opening the junk drawer next to the fridge, she pulls out a Chinese takeout menu. Scanning it, she finds a few entrées she can reheat over the next few days, pushing her trip to the grocery store out past Wednesday.

Hanging up the phone, her packed suitcase looms in the corner of the kitchen. "Ugh." She exhales a sharp breath. "Crap." She continues to mumble as she unpacks it, throwing everything into the wash in one load. She zips it closed and sets it next to the washer.

She hears the muffled ring of her cell phone. Patting herself down, she searches the counter and her purse. "Where are you?" She follows the sound, leading her to the couch. Digging between the cushions, she finds it buried at the bottom. "Hello?"

"Listen, you bitch. You got me fired."

She looks at the caller ID. Unknown number. "Who is this?"

"You know who I am. I'm going to sue you."

"Thomas? Is that you?" She holds her phone out and puts it on speaker, then pushes the button to record the call. "Why are you calling me? I didn't have anything to do with you being fired."

"Yes, you did. You told Jane about the offer. You didn't have to go and tell her. This is what I get for looking out for you."

Chandra's jaw hangs open. "Excuse me? How were you looking out for me by trying to trick me into leaving Baker and Son?"

"Montreux offered you a huge contract. But out of some loyalty to Jane and Baker you screwed me over."

"I found out what you were doing. If I left and went to Montreux, you were going to get a sweet bonus. Not my fault you actually thought I would leave."

"You won't get away with it. I'm suing you, Jane, and the company. I'll do whatever it takes to ruin you. I won't let you get away with this, Chandra. You're the one I blame."

Chandra stares at the silent phone. Her heart thuds in her chest. Her trembling fingers make it next to impossible for her to hit the right buttons on her phone. She takes a deep breath, settling herself down, then dials Jane.

"Chandra, I'm about to leave the office. What's up?"

"Jane, Thomas phoned me and threatened to ruin me. I recorded the call."

"Okay. Okay. I need you to take a deep breath. I promise you he's trying to keep you from giving your statement to the court."

Chandra runs a hand through her hair. "What statement? I wasn't aware I had to give a statement."

"Oh honey, I'm sorry. I found out from the lawyers today we would all need to give statements to combat his lawsuit. I forgot to tell you. I should've warned you he might try to contact you."

Chandra remembers the dead animal in her trash. "When did he find out we would be giving statements?"

"I'm not sure," Jane pauses. "I think two days ago. No, early Monday. Yes, yesterday."

A slight wave of relief washes over her. It must have been Thomas. "I think he put a dead animal in my trash sometime late Monday night."

"What? Are you serious? Do you have him on camera?"

Chandra's brow wrinkles. "No, unfortunately I don't have a security system. I never thought he would resort to this."

"Has he done anything else?"

"I'm not sure. I had something happen last night. I'm sure Thomas had something to do with it. I wonder if he sent those flowers to me as well."

"I could see the dead animal. Sounds like something he would do to threaten you. Although, I don't see him sending you flowers. Plus, I thought Adam sent those."

"No, he didn't. Do you think I have anything to worry about?"

"I really don't believe so. I think if Thomas put the dead animal in your garbage, he did it to scare you. Possibly keep you from doing anything with the case."

"I don't know, Jane. Maybe I should call off the tour. Or at least postpone it for a bit." Chandra paces her living room. Pausing at her front window, she peeks out from behind the curtains.

"I wish we could, but the dates have been set and people are expecting you. I'll arrange for security to travel with you."

"Jane, I don't…"

"Listen, Chandra. I recognize how uncomfortable you are at the thought of doing this tour. But this tour is a must. Baker and Son have a lot riding on you. I'll keep you safe. You don't have anything to worry about concerning Thomas. I'll call the lawyers and let them know what happened. Someone will probably call you tomorrow."

"I still don't…." Chandra says.

"I have to go. I'll call you in the morning with details. Don't worry, Chandra. Okay?"

"Okay. I guess." Chandra stands at the window. A car is driving down the lane. Her heart speeds up until she sees the delivery sign on the roof.

"Talk to you in the morning."

The loud knock on the door makes her jump. She blows out a breath. "Coming," she yells. She quickly signs the receipt, making sure to add in a tip. Thanking the delivery guy, she shuts and bolts the door. Before heading to the kitchen, she pulls the heavy drapes on the front window shut.

Chapter Twelve

Wednesday morning

Chandra races through her house. "I can't afford to be late."

Theo looks up from his bowl. His whiskers covered in moist kitty food.

Rolling her eyes, she bends down and scratches his head. "I'll be back by lunchtime."

Theo growls as he continues eating his salmon feast.

Driving out of her garage, she waits for the door to close. Chandra frowns as she looks at her neighbor putting out his garbage bin. "Oh crap," she says slamming the car into park. She rushes to the side of the house. Careful to stay away from the dead animal she rolls the bin to the curb.

Her stomach growls as she turns onto the main boulevard leading to the library. "I need a coffee." Scanning the stores and restaurants lining the road, Chandra searches for some place to buy a cup of liquid pick-me-up.

"Yes." Chandra reaches for her wallet as she pulls into the drive-through of the Coffee Bean. Ordering a large mocha cappuccino and a blueberry muffin, she maneuvers back into traffic. Her phone pings. "Dang," she says as she realizes she didn't hook it up to the Bluetooth.

Chandra sighs as she drives into the library parking lot. Her dash clock says she has ten minutes. Savoring her muffin, she enjoys the silence and her breakfast, as she checks her messages.

I hope the library group goes well.

"Hmm," she says taking a bite of her muffin. "I wonder who this is." The number is listed as private. Her throat seizes with dryness, making it hard to swallow her bite. Closing her eyes and breathing in and out through her nose, she takes a drink of her coffee. She hasn't given her number to anyone in this group, although that doesn't mean they couldn't have gotten it.

Wrapping up the rest of her muffin, she sips her coffee. "Quit thinking the worst. It's probably just Gretchen." Closing her eyes and resting her head, she takes a few moments to relax. Exhaling slowly, she grabs her coffee and her bag. With three minutes to spare, she goes inside to meet with her group of writers. Roped into this monthly meeting by Jane after Baker and Son published her first book, it's now one of her favorite things to do. "Hello, Merna."

The older lady behind the counter looks up. "Chandra, I'm glad to see you." Merna rushes out to hug her. "A month is too long between your visits." She steps back, holding the author at arm's length. "You look very tired, dear. Have you been sleeping?"

Chandra smiles, nodding. "Yes. Probably not as much as I should."

"Then you're working too hard." Merna takes her hand. "You have some new people here today. People are finding out you hold this meeting, and they want to know all about you and your writing career."

"This isn't supposed to be about me. I want to help other writers."

Merna pats her hand. "Honey, even if a few of them are here to meet you, the majority are here to learn how to make writing a career. Don't let the fame seekers ruin it for you or the others."

Chandra's eyes dart around. She looks over her shoulder, scanning the library. "You said a few new people are here." She turns back to Merna. "Do you know them? I mean—are they regulars to the library?"

Merna frowns, shaking her head as she leads Chandra to the meeting room. "I didn't recognize them. I think it's a couple of men and one young girl." She shrugs. "I'm not sure. There could be more." Stopping at the door, Merna pulls Chandra's hand towards her chest. "I think what you're doing for these writers is wonderful.

Not many famous authors take time out of their day to help people, especially with no pay check in it for them."

"This group has saved me once or twice." Chandra winks at Merna. "I think I'm getting the better deal."

"Well, I'll leave you to it. Enjoy."

Chandra watches Merna stop to help someone find a book. She's reminded of her mother and her job at the library. A rush of memories floods her thoughts. Her love for writing came from all the time spent at the library, reading and escaping. It made her who she is now.

Pushing open the door, several people look up. Many beam smiles and wide eyes at her, blanketing her in a cloak of awkwardness. She finds Gretchen at the front of the room and makes a beeline for her, smiling at a few visitors as she rushes past.

"Gretchen, I'm sorry I'm running a little behind." Chandra places her bag on the table.

"You're right on time. I think most people showed up early." Gretchen gives her a hug. "Did you have a nice weekend?"

"I did."

"And the book signing, did it go well?"

Chandra nods. "Very well. The store had a big turnout."

"I'm glad. I know you didn't want to go away for the weekend."

"I didn't. And I'm happy to be home."

Gretchen glances at the clock on the wall. "Are you ready? I'll introduce you."

Chandra smiles, nodding.

Gretchen faces the large crowd. Mostly older women and men, with a few college-aged students in the mix. "Everyone, I would like to welcome you to this month's Writing with Willis. At last month's meeting, we decided to hold a Q&A this month. Chandra thought it might be time to answer specific questions to help each of you in your writing career." She looks at Chandra. "Without further ado, here is Ms. Chandra Willis."

The room erupts in clapping and a few whistles.

"Okay, okay. That's not necessary. Quick background, I spent most of my junior high and teenage years in a library. My mother happened to be the head librarian. I spent every day after school reading. Doing this writing group is really my way of paying back."

Thankful she didn't need to wear a microphone, the acoustics carried her voice, Chandra takes a small breath. "Who has the first question?" She glances around the room as several raise their hands. Smiling at a young college girl in the back, she points to her. "Yes?"

"Hi, Ms. Willis. First, I have read all your books."

"Thank you," Chandra says.

"My question is, how did you get picked up by a publisher and what do you recommend someone do to increase their chances of getting a deal with a publisher?"

"Wow. That's a great question. Hmm. I didn't set out to be a writer. I actually went to college to be a librarian, like my mother. I wanted to be around books." Chandra walks around the front of the room. "I had no idea I could be a writer. While in college, I entered a short story contest. I used writing to clear my head, take a break from my college studies. Mainly for fun, though. A few of my colleagues read some of my stories, and one of my teachers encouraged me to enter a short horror story I'd written."

Chandra stops pacing. She caught the eye of one of the long-time members of the group. "I hadn't shown it to anyone else. I didn't have it edited, I just sent it in. I got lucky, and it came in second. But the magazine that ran the contest wanted to run my story along with the first and third place winners. I said sure. After that, the same magazine asked me for another short story for their horror anthology. That's where I got my start.

"My story is a little different. From writing for the anthology, I got noticed by an agent. The one I currently have. She asked me to write a full-length novel and submit it to her. For you or anyone else starting out, submit your work to contests. Especially short story contests."

She glances around the room. "Make sure you do the best you can on grammar, maybe get a friend to read it before you submit it. Entering contests is a great way to get more experience under your belt. The best advice I can give is to read. Read books on the craft of writing. Read all genres. Learn what a story arc is. See how different authors approach the craft. Make sure you're hitting what the readers of that genre expect." Chandra walks towards the young girl who asked the question. "Are you in a critique group?"

She shakes her head.

"Get in one," she says, walking back to the front. "A critique group allows you to get your writing in front of people. You need feedback. Honest feedback. When your story is complete, you'll have to research what agents accept your genre.

"Before you send in a query letter, make sure your manuscript is as well edited as you can get it. If you can't pay for an editor, find an English major or English teacher to at least correct your grammar." Chandra smiles. "Does that answer your question?"

"Yes, Ms. Willis it does."

She narrows in on the young girl. "From this point forward, please call me Chandra. That goes for everyone," she says, scanning the room. "Now, who else has a question?"

Several people raise their hands.

"You," she says, pointing to a middle-aged man.

"If you hadn't gotten picked up by the agent the way you did, would you have ever queried your work? Or maybe you would have self-published?"

"Hmm. I probably would've continued to write. I enjoy it. It helps me deal with my anxiety and stress. I like to think I may have queried agents. I don't know if I would have the guts to self-publish."

She leans against the table. "I'm in awe of those who publish their own works. They do everything themselves. I'm lucky I have an agent who handles most things for me. However, on the flip side, I have no control over my covers, or where and when I have a book signing. I go and do what they say."

An older woman raises her hand. "You don't get any say in what the book looks like?"

Chandra shakes her head. "Not really. I can offer some ideas. In the end the publisher is going to go with what they think will sell the most books." She giggles. "Most of my thoughts on my book covers come from the emotional stake I have in the book. I'm not very good with the business side of books. For me, this situation works."

"Has being a writer made you wealthy?"

Chandra eyeballs the older gentleman who asked the question. "I've been very lucky. My books came out at the right time, right place, and I got lucky with a great publisher. Am I dripping in diamonds? Not hardly. Has it provided a nice life? Yes."

She stands silent for a moment. "If you're writing to get rich, that's okay. Some people write what is hot in the market, make tons of money and move on to the next hot book market. I don't hold that against anyone. For me, I write because I need an escape." Chandra's face softens. "I lost my mother while in college. I had a hard time and I used my writing to take away the stress of my ordinary life."

She steps over to the man who asked the question. "Making money is great. Paying for your bills, not worrying about the rent, I get it. Here are my thoughts. Writing what makes you happy, what brings you hope, or joy, is what makes you a successful writer. Or maybe a more fulfilled writer."

Chandra feels her eyes fill with moisture. Blinking, she tries to stymie the tears. "Listen to me. Write what you want, how you want. Just do it. Don't be afraid to share it. Don't take criticism to heart. Don't give up when someone says no."

She looks at everyone in the room. "I'm really grateful I got published by a big publisher. I have a good deal and I know I have more books that will be published. But at the end of the day, there are times I wish I could go back. I'm not sure I would do this again. You lose a lot of freedom.

"My books now have to meet what the publisher thinks will sell, so I often have to change characters or events because they don't like the way they're written." She sighs. "I have to interact and meet new people all the time. Go to events and basically be who they want me to be. I miss the days when no one knew who I was." She smiles, feigning a laugh. "Okay, enough pity party for me."

Gretchen stands, walking towards Chandra. "Our esteemed author has a book signing tonight. I want her to have time to get prepared. I think we can do another session like this next month." She glances at Chandra. "Would that work for you?"

"Oh, I think…" she sighs. "No. I'm going on a six-week tour of the east coast." Chandra glances around the room. "See, no control. I go where they send me."

Several people in the room chuckle.

"I won't be here for next month." She snaps her fingers. "I have an idea. What if we have an online critique session of our work?"

A few soft gasps fill the room.

"For those who want to participate, email Gretchen your work, she will forward it out to everyone who wants to participate," Chandra turns to the assistant librarian. "If you will then forward them to me, I'll read each one and offer comments and suggestions. This will give everyone a chance to have their work read, and when I get back, we can have several critique sessions, going over in person what we do digitally. How does that sound?"

Several people high five each other, while others wiggle in their seats. A resounding yes fills the room.

"Great. Let's set a limit of fifteen thousand words. Pick any part of your story you want to share," Chandra says.

"Where is your book signing tonight?"

Chandra's gaze shifts from face to face. "Who asked that?"

A young man raises his hand. "I did."

She studies the man. Nothing looks familiar about him. "It will be at the Book Nook. It starts at seven." She glances around the room. "You're all welcome to come. I would be thrilled to see all of you there." She nods at several who come up and shake her hand. Exchanging pleasantries, as a shawl of anxiety wraps around her. Watching the last one leave, she turns to Gretchen. "I probably put a lot of work on you, didn't I?"

Gretchen laughs. "Yes, but I don't mind. The looks on their faces when you said you would read their stories, is worth the work load."

"I can use the distraction on the trip. Traveling that long will take a toll on my creativity. Again, I'm sorry if I put you in a bind. Email me everything. I can handle it."

Gretchen touches her forearm. "It isn't a problem. I can create a secure folder everyone can access on Google Docs. Only those in this group will have access."

As they near the doors, Gretchen reaches out, stopping Chandra. "Is there anything wrong?"

Chandra tries not to withdraw. She ignores the urge to run through the door. "No. Why do you ask?"

"You seem a little off. Usually you're more excited about talking with the group. This morning, not so much."

"Oh, no! I hope I didn't make the others feel like I didn't want to be here."

Gretchen shakes her head. "Not at all. You just seem like you're carrying a weight. Like something is bothering you. I'm here to listen, if you ever need an ear."

"I appreciate your offer. I guess this trip has me a little worried. I hate being away from my home. I hate going to all these hotels and inns. I guess my anxiety is getting the best of me."

They walk out the conference room doors.

"I'll be here or at home, if you ever need me. Chandra, I want you to think of me as a friend. I consider you one. We have spent too many hours together here at the library to not be friends."

Chandra hugs her. "I do think of you as a friend. And don't be surprised when I take you up on the offer." She lifts her wrist, not seeing the numbers on her watch. "I have to run. I have a bunch to do for the meet and greet tonight." She rolls her eyes. "I'm doing a private party for the owner of the shop first, then the open book signing." She heads towards the main entrance, almost in a run. "I'll call you. Thank you, Gretchen." She turns to leave, then spins back around. "Did you text me this morning?"

Gretchen shakes her head. "No. Why?"

"Nothing. See you in a couple of months."

"Wait!" Gretchen holds up a finger. "I almost forgot. Someone left something for you in the drop box this morning." She shuffles through a folder. "Here." She holds it out.

Reaching for the card, Chandra's hand trembles. "Do you know who left it?"

Gretchen shakes her head. "No. Like I said it was in the drop box. We have a place for people to make payments for fines if the library is closed. That's where I found it this morning."

Chandra shrugs. "I have no idea why anyone would leave a note in the box."

"Maybe they wanted to come to the meeting but couldn't, so they left a note." Gretchen reaches out to her. "Are you sure you're okay?"

Chandra nods. "Yeah. I'm okay. Just overwhelmed. Thank you for this." She waves as she exits the building.

Gretchen watches her friend run out the door. She wonders what has her frazzled. Sighing, she walks back to her desk. An uncomfortable feeling settles around her. She stares out the doors as a knot begins to form deep in her belly.

Chapter Thirteen

Chandra sits in her car, staring at the envelope. She starts to open the card, deciding against it. She drops it in her purse. She drives to the entrance and pulls into a parking space. Curiosity gets the best of her. She removes the card. Staring at it, she takes a deep breath, then opens the envelope.

Chandra, I couldn't make this meeting. But I look forward to seeing you soon. I hope you like my surprise in the meantime.

She looks at the front, it just has her name. The card isn't signed. She blows out a few sharp breaths. "What surprise?" The question comes out as a whine. Rereading the card, it's not threatening. "If I told anyone, they'd be like, you're crazy Chandra."

She pulls out of the library. The ride to her home is fairly short. The traffic is light, and she finds herself creeping past the speed limit. She thinks back to the meeting, trying to remember everyone's face and name. Recalling the new attendees, she can't remember ever seeing any of them at her signings.

However, after a while, the people blur together. Flexing her fingers and doing shoulder rolls to ease the tension, she breathes slowly. Over the past few months, she can't recall anyone at the meetings being overly friendly. "What freaking surprise?' she yells out.

Slowing her breathing, she has to get ahold of her anxiety before tonight's party, or everyone will be questioning her. "Get yourself together." She mumbles as she pulls into her drive. Something off to her left catches her eye. A quick glimpse at her front door has her heart thudding against her chest. Pulling into the garage, she slams the car into park. Leaving everything, she jumps out.

Walking at a brisk pace, the click clack of her shoes echoes between her ears. Her front porch is now in view. "Oh my gosh!" her hand covers her mouth. "No, no, no." Her fingers reach out, touching a pedal. Another bouquet of all pink flowers fills her entire doorway.

Looking over one shoulder, then the other, she inspects every inch of her street and neighbor's homes. Nothing looks out of place. Rushing into her garage, she grabs her purse, keys, and phone. She waits to open the mudroom door until the garage door closes.

Entering her home, Theo greets her. Ignoring him, she throws her things on the kitchen table before rushing to the front door. Picking up the newest bouquet, she sets it on her entryway table. Locking her front door, she leans against it. Her shaking hand reaches out for the card. She pulls it back as if her fingers were singed by a flame. Chandra closes her eyes, taking a deep calming breath. She carries the vase to the kitchen table.

Theo nudges her leg.

Bending over, she picks him up, burying her face in his fur. "Theo, I'm sorry I didn't say hello." She kisses his nose and puts him back down. Feeling calm, she picks out the card from its holder. A slight tremble starts at her finger tips. As she reads the card, the trembling moves across her entire body.

Pink really is your color. Love, your biggest fan.

She rushes to the security phone on the wall.

"Front gate."

"This is Chandra Willis…"

"Yes, Ms. Willis. What can I do for you?"

"Can you tell me who delivered the flowers I found on my front porch?"

"Hang on a moment."

Chandra hears the man flipping through paper. Her foot taps the tile floor.

"Ms. Willis?"

"Yes, I'm here."

"I don't show any delivery to your house today."

She shakes her head. "Then how did a huge bouquet get on my doorstep?"

"I have no idea. I don't have any record of anyone even visiting you or requesting entry on your behalf. Could one of your neighbors have left it?"

Tears swell over the edges of her eyes. "Why would any of my neighbors give me flowers? Are you sure you don't have any record of a florist coming in for another house and delivering them to me as well?"

"No. I'm sorry. I don't. I don't see any other way someone could gain entry into the community. It has to be one of your neighbors, or someone who lives in the community."

Her free arm wraps around her stomach. "Thank you. Oh, one more thing. Can you remove Thomas Rheingold from my list of approved visitors?"

"I can do that."

"Also, out of curiosity, do you show Thomas coming into the neighborhood anytime this week?

"No. I'm looking through the log. To be honest, if they are on your list, we don't usually make a note."

She sighs. "Thank you again." Hanging up the phone, she reaches into her back pocket for her cell.

"Hey, Chandra. What's up?"

"Adam, you remember those flowers I thought you delivered to the radio station?"

"Yeah, why?"

"Today when I came home from the library, I had another bouquet on my front door step."

"Chandra, I'm not understanding the importance. You got another bouquet? I'm not sure why getting flowers is such a bad thing."

"I'll tell you what the problem is," she picks up the card off the table, "this is what the card said… *Pink really is your color. Love, your biggest fan.* That's what the damn problem is."

"Chandra, you have to calm down."

"Please don't tell me to calm down. This is serious. He left a note at the library."

"Now you've lost me."

She growls into the phone. "Someone left me a note this morning at the library. I got it at the end of the meeting."

"Okay, great someone from your writers group gave you a card."

"NO! The card said *Chandra, I couldn't make this meeting. But I look forward to seeing you soon. I hope you like my surprise in the meantime.* Then another bouquet shows up with reference to pink being my color. I wore pink to the radio station. That means he must be following me."

"Chandra, please. It's…"

"Never mind. Just forget I mentioned it." She realizes how crazy she sounds.

"No. I'm not going to forget it. Let's think about this. First take a deep breath. You need to relax. I think you're getting too worked up over this."

"Easy for you to say. It's not your life."

"Chandra. Think about this. All of these events don't need to be connected. They could be completely independent of each other."

"That doesn't make sense."

"Yes, it does. Let's take the new bouquet. They were left at your door. If we use the card from the library, this must be the surprise they were talking about. Somehow they had the flowers delivered to your home."

"The guard shack said there was no record of a delivery today."

"Doesn't mean there wasn't one. A friend of mine lives in a gated community. People pay the guards off all the time."

"What about the other bouquet. Who delivered those?"

"Another fan. You would not believe how many gifts some people get from fans."

"I don't have that many fans."

"You'd be surprised."

"What about the dead animal in my trash?"

"Thomas or your neighbor."

"Why would the neighbor do that?"

"To rattle you. You snub him all the time. Maybe he just wants to mess with you. You have said he has become a little more aggressive in trying to talk to you. Maybe he's tired of you ignoring him. He put the dead animal in your trash. He figures this is a good way to get into your head.”

“He didn't leave the note at the library. How do you explain that away?”

“I told you, separate incident. Your meetings at the library aren't top secret. Hell, the library runs a monthly ad about it. Whoever left that note, is a fan and wanted to give you flowers. Just like the one from the radio station. I don't know why you threw them out in the first place.”

“I didn't throw them out. When I went to do it, the dead animal was there. I didn't want to touch it. So, I kept them.” Chandra stares out her glass door. Her property used to bring her such a sense of peace and safety. Not now.

“Well, I'm glad to hear that and proud of you for not giving in to your crazy. I think you should enjoy them.” He waits for a response. “Hello? Are you there?”

Adam's voice pulls her out of her trance. “Yeah. I'm here.”

“Sweetie, I know all this exposure is rattling you. I know you have a hard time dealing with this type of notoriety. But you have to learn to take it in stride.”

“I didn't sign up for this. I wanted to write stories. That's it.”

“Well, too late now to go back. You have to enjoy these gifts and quit thinking it's someone bad trying to get to you.” Justin pauses. “I do think, your old grumpy neighbor wants more attention from you. Maybe he sees this hot shot author living next door, and thinks you should be more friendly. You aren't, so he messes with you.”

“What should I do? Say something to him?”

“Nah, when you see him wave, if he tries to talk to you, engage him for a few minutes. I bet if you show him some attention, he will stop.”

“Sure. I guess.” She says the words but her brain is screaming at her. Telling her that isn't what's going on.

“Hey, you want me to pick you up tonight? I can.”

“You wouldn't mind?”

“Not at all.”

“I would appreciate it, Adam. The thought of coming home alone tonight doesn't sound fun.”

"No worries. I'll be there at four. We need enough time to get there and get set up."

"Thank you, Adam. Please don't say anything to Jane. She will think I've lost my mind."

"I won't. It will be our little secret. Try not to worry. I can tell your mind is spinning out of control."

"I'll try not to."

"See you in a few hours. Tell the gate to expect me."

"You're on my list of approved visitors. All you need to do is give them my name."

"Okay. See you soon."

Chandra sets the phone on the table. She wants to believe Adam that the flowers are harmless tokens. They are beautiful. Scary and creepy, too. But something is unnerving about them. Maybe she can learn to enjoy things like this. Theo jumps onto the table; her hand clutches her shirt. "I've got to get a hold of myself, Theo."

The cat head butts her, rubbing his cheek along hers. His purring fills the quiet room.

The clicking of the mantle clock echoes in the otherwise silent house. She lays her head on her left arm and wraps the cat up with the other one, burying her face in his fur as she rubs his belly. Closing her eyes, she wishes for her mom. Growing up, it had been just the two of them, after her father died. Her mother had been a much stronger woman than herself. Chandra knows her mother would have words of wisdom on how to deal with this situation.

"I'm a coward, Theo. Scared of everything. Anxious over things I can't control. I see the worst and not the best."

Theo snuggles against her, rolling more onto his back. When she quits rubbing his belly, he gently uses his paw to get her attention.

"You're my one saving grace. I don't think I would even be functional without you."

A few hours later she sits on her sofa, waiting for Adam. Her knees bounce with the rapid rise and fall of her heels. Theo is laying at the other end of the sofa. He cracks one eye open, as he curls into a tighter ball.

"Don't judge me," Chandra says. She continues to scan her backyard. The glass wall, once an invitation to nature and relaxation, is now a barrier. Standing, she wraps her arms around her waist and moves towards it.

She reaches out for the remote to unlock and open the doors, drawing her hand back. Stepping closer to the door, the hair on the back of her neck bristles. Squinting, her eyes roam over the tree line. She sees no one. Shifting to the left, she leans into the glass with her brow resting against it.

She doesn't see anything at the edge of the deck. Shifting her gaze towards the right, she tries to see the other end. Rubbing her arms, Chandra steps back. "I'm positive I saw movement in the trees." Her voice breaks. She uses the remote to frost the glass, making it solid frost instead of opaque.

The flowers taunt her. She walks to her mudroom and makes sure the door is locked. Satisfied everything is secure, she returns to her living room.

Her purse is on the coffee table. She checks it to make sure she has enough business cards to hand out. Something she does with every book she signs. Her cards have limited information on them. No phone number, only her email and the website her publisher set up for her.

Again, her stare is drawn towards the backyard. She can't see through the frosted glass, but something isn't right; she feels off kilter. Like something is going to go wrong any minute. A slight shiver runs down her spine. "I should've called a security company." She jumps, clutching her chest at the sound of a car horn.

Hurrying to her front window, she peaks under the edge of the drapes. Adam is in her driveway. Making sure she leaves several lights on, she picks up her purse and rushes out the front door. She takes a few steps towards the car, turns around, and double checks the locks.

Chapter Fourteen

"Hi. I'm glad you picked me up," Chandra says, smiling.

"No problem at all. I'm glad to do it. Have you received any more calls today from Thomas?"

"No. Why? Have you heard something?"

Adam chuckles. "No silly. Calm down. I had to give my deposition to one of the in-house lawyers today, a preliminary one. They're trying to find out to what extent they need to deal with him."

Chandra shakes her head. "I don't understand."

"Jane thinks he's doing this to make noise. She and the lawyers don't think he has any standing. Last I heard they're deciding if they should sue him or simply let it go. They want this whole thing to blow over."

Chandra's knee starts bouncing. "This isn't good. If they sue him, he'll blame me for sure."

Adam gives her a sideways glance. "How is that even logical?"

"He's harassing me because he blames me for his firing. Just think what he will blame me for if he is sued. Let alone if he has to pay for damages. That will cost him money. He will blame me, and then what else will he do to me?"

Adam turned off the freeway, heading towards Main St. "Wow. Your brain really thinks the worst."

She sighs.

"Okay. Let's think this through. He has to be aware all eyes are on him. He's pretty much under the microscope when it comes to interacting with anyone from Baker and Son. If he starts doing anything more than phone calls, he'll be in some serious shit."

"I guess, Adam."

"I thought about something this afternoon. What about that neighbor you had the property problem with?"

She frowned at him. "What are you talking about?"

"The neighbor who had a problem with the trees. I can't remember his name. You told me once he complained they encroached onto his property. I remember the situation turned pretty heated between you two. The neighbor on the other side of you."

She waves him off. "Mr. Gardner. We settled. They had marked his line incorrectly." She snickers. "I actually gained three feet into his yard. I waved my standing to the property and had new plot lines made. In the end, I gave him two feet."

"Maybe he's been stewing about it."

Chandra shrugs, leaning her head back. "I guess, but that issue was settled and he came out ahead. I can see if I screwed him and took my three feet back. I don't think Mr. Gardner is so diabolical that he'd mess with my head. He got what he wanted. I don't think he would have any reason to harass me."

Adam parks in front of the book store. He turns towards her. "You never know with some people. He and Mr. Franks has the money to harass you." He takes her hand in his. "Either way, change how you speak to both of them. Be nice. And I bet things change." He winks at her. "Now, let's go in, enjoy the private party. There's food and drinks. The other customers will be here in about two hours. Enjoy tonight and let this take your mind off everything."

"Okay. I could use a distraction." She follows him to the back of the vehicle. As the rear door to the SUV opens, Chandra glances around the street. "I didn't realize the radio station and book store were in the same part of town."

"Oh, yeah. One street over." Adam pulls the foldable dolly out from the back and places several boxes of books on it. "Grab that bag. It has the table top stuff for the signing. We'll get set up before the private party. Then when the doors open to the public, you'll be ready to go."

Chandra grabs the bag, following Adam into the shop. The smell of cinnamon and cloves greet her. Inhaling the odor fills her with memories of her mother's home at this time of year. She closes her eyes and drifts back to a place of calmness and joy.

"Hello? Chandra?" Adam is snapping his fingers in front of her face.

"Uh? What?"

"Where the hell did you go?" He asks, nodding to the table at the back of the store. "I've been calling your name for like an eternity."

"Stop. We just walked through the door."

"Long enough for me to wonder if I needed to call the police. Now quit daydreaming and help me."

Chandra chuckles. "This place reminds me of my childhood home. I want to escape back to that time in my life."

"No escaping. Get to work."

"Damn, you're a slave driver." Chandra unloads the props for the table. A bookstand holds her last five published books, while the newest release is stacked at the end of the table. "Why are we stacking these here? They have to buy their book before they get into line for my autograph."

Adam squints at her. "If we did it your way, there would be one pen and you at the table." He lifts up the banner, securing it to the stand, setting it at the end of the table.

"That's all I need. The readers know what books I have, all this other stuff," she points at the table decorations and stand, "this is all fodder."

"No wonder so many authors make horrible marketers."

Chandra opens her mouth to say something, when a robust man walks up to her. Standing up straight, she brushes off her hands.

"I'm thrilled to have you here." The man extends his hand.

Chandra took it, only to have him wrap her up in a hug. "Uh, oh, okay. Hi. I'm thrilled to be here too. Thank you for having me," she says smiling at him. A quick glance towards Adam brings no relief from her discomfort. Expecting him to save her, he stands there with an ear-to-ear grin, amused at her expense. She looks back to her new best friend. "This is Adam. He's my editor, my agent's right-hand man, and plans all my events."

"Adam, it's nice to put a face to the voice." He shakes his hand. "I'm glad this didn't have to be rescheduled."

"I'm sorry for the mix-up. But we're here now and Chandra," he says motioning to her, "is very excited to be here. She loves these intimate gatherings. Isn't that right, Chandra?"

Nodding, she looks at the shop owner. "I'm very excited. I don't think Adam has told me your name."

"Forgive me. I'm Caleb Jones. I've owned this place for the last fifteen years." He glances over his shoulder. "My wife helps me with the bookkeeping and runs the register when our helper can't be here." His face frowns. "She's dying to meet you in person. I don't know where she is. I expected her to be right over. Do you need any help here?"

Adam shakes his head. "Nope. We're almost done."

Caleb takes Chandra's hand as he checks his watch. "Everyone should be showing up very soon. In the back room, we have food and drinks." He points to the restroom sign above the front desk. "The bathroom is down the hallway behind the counter. Take a few minutes and then come to the back room."

Chandra smiles. "Sounds perfect. I'll go to the restroom and then I'll be right there."

Adam watches Caleb head towards the back. He turns to Chandra. "You ready?"

She nods. "Yeah. I think this party and signing will go a long way to take my mind off things. I'll meet you in a few minutes." She hugs him. "Thanks again for driving me."

"No problem. I'll meet you in there."

Chandra heads to the hallway, admiring several paintings on the wall as she finds her way to the restroom. It's a single. No stalls. She locks the door behind her, grateful for the few minutes of privacy. Washing her hands, she stares at herself in the mirror. Her curls hang loose on her shoulders. Her pale blue eyes stare back at her. Opening them wide and smiling, she hopes the worry they carry won't be noticeable. Trying several facial expressions, she gives up when she hears the doorknob rattle. "Almost done," she yells out. "I'm going to have to smile all night," she whispers.

Exiting, she glances up and down, expecting to see someone waiting to use the restroom. Her brow wrinkles at the empty hallway. A quick glance to her left, she turns right and smacks into a man.

"Excuse me," Chandra says. The greenest eyes are staring back at her. Her heart races, thumping against her chest. Her body trembles and her legs feel like noodles. Chandra takes a step back, glancing around the man's shoulder towards the front of the book store.

"I'm sorry. I should've paid better attention." He smiles, stepping off to the side.

The dim lights are still bright enough to highlight the gold specks in his eyes, causing a sparkle effect. His dark wavy hair is mussed up. He's a good three inches taller and his shoulders look as if he has to turn sideways to get through a doorway. Chandra takes a deep breath to steady herself. "Have I seen you anywhere before?"

His nostrils flare as he walks past her. "I don't know. Have you?" He winks as he enters the restroom.

Chandra rushes to the other room. She wrings her hands as she searches the small crowd of people for Adam. Her hurried gait weaves her through the guests. As she approaches Adam, she reaches out to grab his arm when she's pulled away.

"Ms. Willis…"

Chandra yelps before turning to see Caleb. She exhales as relief washes over her. She raises her hand, lowering it before he notices the shaking. "Please, call me Chandra."

"Chandra, this is my wife, Christine."

Christine is rail thin. Her shiny gray hair is pulled back in a bun at the base of her head. Her eyes are as yellow as a cat's. "Nice to meet you."

Christine grabs her around the neck. "I can't tell you how long I have been waiting for tonight. To get to meet you in the flesh." She steps back. "I enjoy reading your books. You make being scared way too much fun."

Chandra smiles, looking up. The man from the hallway watches her as he moves to the buffet table. "I see more people have shown up."

Caleb nods. "I'm going to introduce you in about…" he looks at his watch, "say about five minutes."

Chandra gives him a thumbs up. "I need to speak with Adam, then I'll be ready to go." She excuses herself and makes a beeline for him. "Hey," she says tapping him on the shoulder.

"Hey, yourself. It looks like it's getting ready to start." He studies her face. "What happened?"

She tugs him into the corner. "I just saw him."

"Saw who?" Adam says as he looks around the room.

"The guy from a few of my signings." The pitch in her voice rises. "He's here." Her voice trembles along with her entire body.

Chapter Fifteen

Adam's eyes widen. "No shit?" He spins around. "Where? Point him out to me."

Chandra stays tucked into the corner of the room, shielding herself behind Adam. "He's there." She points to the table.

Adam's back is to her. "Where?" He asks, as he turns around and follows her finger with his gaze. "Who?"

"The guy at the buffet table."

"There are like three guys at the table. Which one?"

Chandra leans around him and points to the man in the jeans and sweatshirt. "Him."

Adam ogles the man. "He doesn't look like a stalker."

"Oh, for Pete's sake. Do they ever look like a stalker?"

Adam turns around. "Calm down. You can't be sure he's a bad guy or not. Maybe he likes your books."

"No. I'm sure it's him I've seen around." She pinches the bridge of her nose. "At least I think I have." She's about to say something when Caleb taps a glass. "Oh great." She fixes her shirt and runs her fingers through her hair.

"Everyone, I want to thank you for coming to this private signing. For several years now, my wife has crooned about this writer. 'You have to read her books' she would say. So finally, I did. And she's now one of my favorite authors. To have her here for some of my closest friends, brings me more joy than you know. Please let me introduce you to Ms. Chandra Willis."

Applause erupts. Chandra walks through a cleared path of patrons. Moving through the crowd, she keeps her would be stalker in her peripheral vision. "I'm thrilled to be here, and I'm honored you have made time in your day for me," Chandra says, facing the crowd.

Caleb takes her hand. "This is our time with her before the doors open for the remainder of the signing." He points in the direction of a table. "Let's take a few minutes to eat and talk. Feel free to ask Ms. Willis questions, and then she can sign books."

"I don't mind signing books now, either. I'm here for you guys," Chandra says, glancing at Caleb and then the crowd.

"Get a snack, Chandra. The canapés are delicious. Get a drink. Answer questions, then sign." Caleb watches as his wife hands her a small plate of food and a cup of punch.

Chandra smiles, taking them from Christine. "Thank you." She sets her drink down on a table next to her. The man with the green eyes is mingling. He seems comfortable and at ease. Her brow furrows as he periodically looks up and smiles at her, occasionally nodding in her direction.

Adam is standing next to her, watching the man she's convinced is her stalker. "He looks harmless," he says leaning into her ear.

"Chandra, Ms. Willis?"

Chandra's attention is brought back to the woman in front of her. "Pardon me."

The woman smiles. "Julian has that effect on most women."

Chandra swallows a lump of food. "Excuse me?"

"Julian." The woman points to the man across the room. "I'm assuming he's the reason for your distraction."

Chandra can feel the heat rush to her cheeks. "Um, no. I mean, that's not…."

The lady leans back and laughs. "Honey, everyone looks at Julian like that. Why he's not a model, no one will ever know."

"You know him?" Chandra asks.

"Of course, I do. Don't you? Hang on a moment." The woman walks away.

Chandra leans into Adam. "I'm confused," she says, taking a sip of her drink and placing her plate on the table at the same time.

They both watch as the older woman comes back to them.

"She's bringing him over," Chandra says. Her jaw begins to ache. She forces herself to relax, rolling her shoulders to lessen the tension.

"Ms. Willis, this is Julian. Julian Drake."

"Martha, have you introduced yourself to Ms. Willis?" He says without taking his eyes off the author.

"Oh, gosh, I'm sorry. I'm Martha Vantrese. I'm the Mayor of Londonberry." She squints at Chandra. "I know from your bio you grew up in Manchester, what part?"

Chandra's head pounds. Julian's masculine scent fills her nose. She inhales, hoping it lingers. Her stomach flutters as if she swallowed a thousand butterflies. "I'm sorry, what did you ask me?"

Adam steps closer to the group. "Chandra grew up in Chester."

Chandra nods. "Yes. I grew up in Chester. Moved away for a short time when I went to college. Moved back here right after."

Martha wraps her right arm around Julian's waist. "This man grew up here and is currently the lead homicide detective at the Manchester State Police. That and many other things at the department. Weren't you on a special task force for the FBI?"

Chandra's eyes feel as if they're going to pop out of her head. She looks over at Adam, then back at Julian. "You're a detective?"

"Yes. Did you think I was someone else?" Julian asks.

A young girl comes up to the group.

"Well, I…I thought…"

"Ms. Willis?"

Chandra stops speaking and squats down to the little girl's level. "What can I do for you?"

"Would you sign this? I can't wait any longer."

The young girl's mother rushes up to the group. "Please forgive my daughter. I told her she would have to wait until you were done with your food." The mother frowns at the little girl. "Shelby."

"It's okay," Chandra says, taking the book from the little girl. "That's why I'm here—to sign books." She looks at her. "Is there anything special you want me to say in it?"

Shelby's eyes lit up. "Yes please."

"What?" Chandra asks.

"To Shelby, my biggest fan." A big smile pushes her cheeks up high.

"Are you my biggest fan?" Chandra begins to write in the book as she listens to Shelby's response.

"Absolutely. Not only am I your biggest fan, I bet I'm the youngest. I'm ten years old."

Chandra eyeballs the little girl. "Aren't my stories scary?"

The girl's eyebrows raise. "Yes. That's why I love them."

The mother's cheeks turn bright red. "I know I'm a bad mom," she says unable to make eye contact. "She reads on an advanced level, and she found your books on my shelf. She read them all."

Chandra places a hand on the lady's shoulder. "My mother was a librarian. I can't tell you how many books I read that my friends' parents wouldn't even allow in their houses." She hands the book back to Shelby after placing a business card in the center of it. "You email me and tell me what you're doing. I expect to hear what college you decide to attend. And when you're famous, I hope you remember me." She winks at her.

"I promise, Ms. Willis." Shelby's arms wrap around Chandra's waist. "I want to be just like you when I grow up."

Chandra pushes her back, shaking her head. "No."

Shelby's eyes glass over.

"I expect you to be better than me. You understand?"

Shelby giggles. "I'll be better than you. Thank you, Ms. Willis."

"You're welcome." Chandra takes several books from other patrons and signs them. She gives a sideways glance towards the Lieutenant and Adam. They're having an animated chat a few feet away. Another man is lingering near the table. He is reading the back cover of her book. She can't see his face directly but she doesn't recognize him from anywhere. At least she doesn't think so.

Adam and Lieutenant Drake walk over to Chandra.

Lieutenant Drake crosses his arms. "Let me get this straight. You thought I was a stalker?"

Chandra's shoulders droop. "Adam."

"What? I think it's hysterical." Adam places his drink on the table. "I'm going to go out and make sure we're good to go. The doors will open shortly for the crowd outside.

As Chandra stands in front of Julian, a few special guests come over to get their books signed and take pictures with her. She cocks an eyebrow at Julian's amused expression. "I'm glad you think this is funny."

"It's not every day I get accused of being a stalker." Julian steps to the side as the last of the group takes selfies with Chandra. Her features are even more beautiful up close. Her smooth skin, a pale beige, begs to be caressed. She covers her anxiety well. He watches as she interacts with her fans. They have no idea how truly uncomfortable she is in this kind of environment. He can't hide his grin.

Chandra cocks an eyebrow at him. "What's so amusing?"

"Just watching you," Julian says.

"I've seen you at a few of my signings here in town. Right?"

He laughs. "Yes. One, I wanted to get the nerve to talk to you. Two, I wanted to get the nerve to talk to you."

She narrows her eyes. "That's why I thought you were a stalker. Why didn't you buy my book? I would've signed it, and you could've spoken to me."

"Too easy." He follows her to the front of the store.

Chandra walks towards the table. "Hey, Adam, are we ready?"

"Everything is set up," Adam says adjusting the sign behind the table.

Chandra turns to face the Lieutenant. "Can you stay? Maybe you can help me figure out how to handle my would-be stalker." Chandra pulls another chair over near her table. "You can sit here."

Adam nods at Julian. "Yes, stay. We could use some help on what to do." He glances at Chandra. "Or actually what we can do to prove to Chandra she doesn't have a stalker." He wiggles is eyebrows at her.

"What do you think she has?" Julian asks.

"I think she has a superfan or several fans, and a grumpy neighbor. Possibly even a few superfans. Nothing more."

Chandra bites her bottom lip. "It doesn't matter. I'm sure I'm over reacting, but I would still like the help. Could you?"

Julian bows slightly. "Your wish is my command."

Just as she's about to say something, the doors open and the crowd flows in. People rush to the stacks of her books. Some come with books in hand. Not wanting to turn anyone away, Chandra obliges and signs all copies.

"Ms. Willis, I love your books. They keep me up at night," one lady says as she waits for Chandra to sign her book.

"I'm thrilled to hear you say that. Tell me your name."

"Amanda."

Chandra signs the book, handing it back to her. "Thank you for your support, Amanda." Glancing up, the line has thinned considerably. The clock on the wall says nine p.m. She looks around the room before coming back to Julian. "Where's Adam?"

"He received a phone call. Said he would be right back."

Chandra signs the last customer's book. Giving the patron one of her hardback books sitting on the table as a gift, signing it as well.

"What a nice thing for you to do," Julian says, as he stands and stretches.

"I've made it a habit. Whoever is last in line gets a free copy of the hardback book. Don't remember when I started doing it." She begins to pack up the standing banner. Along with the box of remaining hard cover books. "Always less to pack than to unpack."

Caleb and Christine walk over to her. "Chandra, this has been one of the best nights at my book store. I can't thank you enough."

Christine hands her a box of cookies. "These are my special recipe. I wanted to give you something from us."

Chandra lifts the lid off the small tin and sniffs. "These cookies smell wonderful. Thank you."

Adam joins them. "Hey, sorry."

"Anything wrong?" asks Chandra.

"No. I need to go back to the office. I'm closest and Jane left a contract on her desk. She's flying out in the morning to LA."

"Adam, it will take you forever to take me home then drive to the office. I can call a cab." Chandra pulls her phone from her purse.

"Chandra, I can't let you call a cab. I can drop you off, drive over to the office, then head to Jane's." Adam stacks everything on the fold up dolly. Securing it.

"I can take you home," Julian says.

Chandra's butterflies return. "No. No. I can't ask you to drive me home."

Maneuvering the dolly towards the door, Adam says, "What a perfect idea. And a solution to our problem."

"I don't know him." She turns to Julian. "No offense."

"None taken. But technically, I'm not a stranger."

"And he's a cop. How much safer can you be?" Adam asks, shifting his gaze between the two.

Chapter Sixteen

Sweat beads at the base of Chandra's hairline. "I really don't think...."

Martha Vantrese walks up to the small group. "Well, I'm off." She turns to Julian, reaching out to take him in a hug. "Tell your parents, I said hello. And I expect to see them at the City Council meeting next week."

Julian brushes his lips against her cheek as he winks at Chandra. "I will tell them, Martha."

Martha turns to Chandra. "What a pleasure to meet you in person, young lady. Keep the wonderful stories coming." She wraps her scarf around her neck.

Adam holds the door for her.

Chandra grabs her purse from under the table. "Adam, can I help you take the books out to the car?"

Adam rolls the boxes out the door. Turning around, he shakes his head. "Nope, I got it. I'll call you tomorrow." He nods at Julian. "Thanks for taking her home."

Julian turns to Chandra. "Am I taking you home?"

Chandra's eyes dart to Adam, who is now at the back of his vehicle. She looks for Caleb or Christine, but they seem to have vanished into the back of the store.

"Well?" Julian asks, gesturing towards the door. "I don't bite, you know?"

A weak smile pulls her lips back. "Are you sure you don't mind?" she asks following his extended arm towards the door.

"Not at all." He pulls the door open. "Your chariot awaits."

Chandra chuckles. "Oh, brother."

Julian follows her out onto the sidewalk. "What, can't a man be chivalrous these days?"

"I don't know what that is."

"What…what is?" Julian asks as he points to his car at the end of the block.

"A chivalrous man. I think they're almost extinct," Chandra says.

Using the key fob to unlock the passenger side door, he opens it for her. "My, we're a tad bit cynical, aren't we?" He closes the door walking around the front of the vehicle to the driver's side.

"It's nice and warm in here. How did you start the car?"

He holds up his key ring. "Remote start. You should've worn a jacket."

"I always forget. Until it gets really cold, anyway."

"Now, about you being cynical."

Chandra giggles. "I'm not really. I guess I haven't been out with anyone recently to experience all this," she says.

"All what?"

"Opening doors. Giving damsels in distress a ride home."

Julian pulls away from the curb. "Where am I taking you?"

"I live in Chantilly Estates."

Julian whistles. "Fancy."

Chandra frowns at him. "What are you implying?"

He laughs. "I'm kidding. It's a nice place. I didn't know writing paid well enough to live there."

"I didn't know being a detective paid well enough to buy a high-end luxury car."

"Things aren't always as they seem."

She turns to him. "What do you mean?"

"I bought it at a police auction."

She huffs. "Anyway, writing doesn't pay well." She crosses her arms. "And you're right, things aren't always as they seem. I mean, don't get me wrong, I got a pretty damn good publishing deal. Not enough to buy my place, and I'm not rolling in money."

"How did you afford it?"

"When my mother died, she left me a small amount of money. Enough to buy the smallest house in the community."

"Why there?"

She shrugs. "I don't know."

Julian flashes a quick smile. "You do remember I'm a detective, right?"

She laughs. "Okay, okay. I like the location and the security." She shakes her head. "Well, at least I thought it had the best security."

Julian maneuvers the car onto the freeway. "What has happened to make you change your mind? Tell me everything."

Chandra turns to stare out her window.

"Chandra? Is something wrong?"

She sighs. "You'll just laugh at me. Or think I'm crazy. Like Adam and everyone else."

"Again, I remind you, I'm a detective. Maybe I can help."

Chandra shifts in her seat. She watches him as he drives. "I don't even know." A nervous laugh escapes. "I thought you were my stalker. Obviously, I'm a nut case."

"You now know it isn't me. Tell me what has you so rattled."

Chandra explains the recent events. She can still smell the dead animal as she tells him about it in her bin. She tugs on the ends of her sleeves, sitting in silence as she waits for the burst of laughter.

Julian takes the exit leading to her neighborhood. "Do you know which neighbor may have put the animal in your trash?"

"No clue. I keep to myself. I hardly speak to anyone. Jane, my agent thinks it could be Thomas."

"Who is Thomas?"

"He's my former editor. He's been fired. He blames me."

"That could be a way for him to get back at you."

"And, I hadn't removed him from my approved list of visitors. So, at the time it happened, he still had access to my neighborhood. The time line also makes sense."

"Have you taken him off the visitors list?"

She nods. "Yes."

"Okay. That should make it harder for him to get in."

"Harder for him to get in? I thought he wouldn't be able to get in at all."

"Anyone can get into a gated community. Takes a little ingenuity, but it can be done."

"Adam told me about guards being bribed." She blows out a breath. "I guess I need to realize I can't live in my little cocoon."

"Don't like being in the limelight, huh?"

"No. I really don't."

"Do you have a security system?"

She shakes her head. "No. One of the guards at the front gate has a list for me. I keep forgetting to get it from them."

"I have someone who can help you." He turns to look at her. "If you want my help."

"I guess. Although I don't know what good it will actually do."

"Catch someone in the act, for one. If you put up a system with flood lights, if anyone comes near your home, the lights will trip on, flooding the area with light." Julian pulls up to her gate.

"Punch in 2768."

He flashes an evil grin. "Telling a stranger your gate code. Shame, shame."

Her eyes narrow in on him. "They change the code weekly. They will change this one," she cocks her head to the side. "Sunday, I think."

"Wow," he says, punching in the numbers on the keypad. "How do you keep up with the code changes?"

"The residents have a bar code on their windshields. The codes are for back up, instances like this. Most in here have a list of approved visitors or add someone when needed. They send out a message with the new code."

Driving through the gate, Julian admires the homes. "These are nice."

"Where do you live?"

"In Londonberry." He pulls into her drive. "Your home is quaint, compared to the other mansions in this place."

Chandra's laughter fills the car.

"What did I say?"

"I have never had my house described as quaint." Containing her laughter, muffled giggles escape. "I think it fits perfectly." She sighs as she catches her breath. She sits up in her seat. "That's strange."

The soft lights around her mailbox illuminate the area enough for her to see something is attached to the door.

Julian looks around. "What's strange?"

"Something is on my mailbox." Chandra jumps from the car, racing to the walkway.

Chapter Seventeen

A red bow is tied around the door latch. She reaches out to open the door, and changes her mind.

Julian walks up next to her. "Well?"

She looks at him, then back at the handle. "There's a bow."

"Was it there earlier?"

"No. And I didn't put it there."

"Did I say you did?"

She crosses her arms. "No. But I can tell from that look that you think I'm stupid."

Julian lifts his hands in the air. "Whoa, I never said or implied you were stupid."

"Your smirk says otherwise. One of the guards gave me the same look."

"I'm not the guards. Open it."

She hesitates then pulls the door open. A small box wrapped in a red ribbon sits in the center. Her hand trembles as she pulls it out. "Great."

"Let's take it inside and open it." Julian holds his arm out.

Chandra walks to her front door unlocking it. Theo scampers out from the living room to greet her. She places her purse on the entryway table, along with the gift.

Theo bypasses her to rub against Julian's leg. "Hey buddy." He picks him up. "Great cat."

She takes him from his arms. "He is. He loves attention."

Julian lifts the box. "Open it."

She glares at him. "I don't want it. Whatever it is."

"Let's see what it is." He holds it out to her.

"Fine." She places Theo on the floor. Taking the box from him, she pulls the ribbon off, lifting the top. Inside on a small leather choker is a silver half heart. She lifts it up. "I don't want this."

Julian pulls the card from the box. He reads it and hands it to her.

"What does it say?" she asks.

"Read it."

Flipping the small card open. Her breath stops.

You will always have a piece of my heart.

She places both back in the box and puts it in the small drawer of the entry table. "This isn't a fan. This is from a stalker. I know it."

"Well. It's not threatening enough on its own. Keep it though. And keep anything else you get from your fan. This way, we can build a pattern of harassment."

"What good will that do?" Her arms flail out. "You just said this isn't threatening. Just like the flowers sitting on my kitchen table. None of it, on its own is threatening. If I took all this to someone, the police or the guard shack, everyone would think I'm nuts." She storms into the kitchen. "My agent and editor, probably the entire publishing company, think I'm a basket case."

Chandra grabs a bottle of wine from the fridge. "I called the guards and told them about someone in my backyard. They didn't believe me."

"These are the flowers you got?"

"One is from the radio station, and one showed up at my door."

"Tell me about someone in your yard."

She lifts the bottle of wine. "Would you like some?"

"Sure."

She opens it while she talks. "I came home from my trip. When I came inside, I had Adam on the phone. We were going over tonight's book signing. Standing in front of the glass doors, I thought I saw a man in my trees." She sips her wine as she continues to tell him the story.

Julian frowns at her. "There's something else. What is it?"

She looks down at her glass. "You won't believe me. You will think I'm crazy, stupid, or forgetful."

"Humor me."

"When I pulled into my garage, the light was on."

"And?"

"And what? That's it. My garage light was on. I never leave my light on. At least I'm pretty sure I don't."

"You think whoever put the dead animal in your bin, got into your house, or at least into your garage, and left the light on?"

"See why I didn't want to say anything?"

"Did Thomas ever have a key to your home?"

She shakes her head. Her eyes widen. "Crap. Yes. He did. I completely forgot about that." She snaps her fingers. "Wait, I got it back from him. Just before he was fired." She flops into a chair at the table. "This is too much."

"Let's look at this." He sips his wine. "I think you have a few different things going on. One, I think Thomas did put the animal in your trash. That may have even been whom you saw in your yard. I think the flowers are from someone else."

She points towards the front door. "And the gift?"

"I think the same person gave you the gift and the flowers." Julian looks at the frosted glass. "Don't you want to see out your door?" he asks pointing to it.

Grateful for the momentary distraction she grabs the remote from the little table. "Watch this." She pushes a button, holding it down until the frosted glass becomes clear. "Pretty cool, huh?"

"It is." He stares out the large window. "Your yard is beautiful."

Chandra smiles at him. "I used to love going out on my deck. I would light the gas firepit, snuggle up with a glass of wine and enjoy nature."

"Why don't you like it anymore?"

She stares out the window before answering. "I don't feel safe. I sometimes feel as if I'm being watched."

"How long has that been going on? That feeling?"

Chandra sighs. "For a while now."

"Did it start when the gifts started?"

"No. It's been going on for longer than that. Which is why the gifts bother me so much."

Julian leans across the table. "Is there anything else, any event, that happened which coincides with the uncomfortable feelings?"

She fiddles with the hem of her shirt. "I had more personal appearances to attend. More meet and greets to do. Radio interviews. I think those feelings started when my schedule increased."

Julian's face softens. "Please don't take this the wrong way. But I think your anxiety and fear about public appearances has you hyper aware of things."

Her bottom lip quivers. She rolls it under her teeth. She stares at her hands before replying. "You basically think I'm crazy, too?"

"No. Not at all. I think your fear and anxiety are quite real. And I think it's making you think irrationally."

She hangs her head. "So, this gift—I shouldn't worry about it?"

"I didn't say that. But I don't think you should jump to the worst possible scenario."

Chandra stands, putting the wine in the fridge.

"Chandra, what else has Thomas done?"

"Don't worry about it."

"Stop."

She looks up. The hair on her arms stands on end. "Why are you angry?"

Julian's lips form a tight line. "I'm not. I'm trying to help."

"He called me. Told me he wanted to get even with me for having him fired. Jane said not to worry. She thinks he's mad because the publishing company is going after him for harassment."

Julian pulls a small notebook from his back pocket. "Tell me his full name."

"Thomas Rheingold."

He jotted a few notes down. "I'll look into him."

Chandra's eyes widen. "I would rather you didn't. If he thinks I sicced you on him, he will only ramp it up. I want it left alone. I don't want you doing anything."

"Chandra, we need to look at him and make sure he isn't capable of anything else. I don't think he is sending the gifts. I think Thomas is the one making threatening calls and trying to stop you from testifying."

"Fine." She picks up the empty wine glasses. "What do you plan to do?" She places them in the sink. Turning towards him, she crosses her arms.

Julian smiles at her. "I'll check on him. See if he has a record. See if I can track his whereabouts without anyone suspecting anything. I will also look and see if any other women from this community has complained of being harassed, just in case. That way we can rule out someone creepy targeting this area. You know, detectivy kinds of stuff."

"Is that a word? Detectivy?"

"It's my word." He stands and moves in front of her. "I promise. We'll figure out what's going on." He reaches out to her, sliding his hand up and down her arm.

Chandra slips out from between him and the counter. "I appreciate any help," she says, walking into the living room.

Julian admires her shape as she slinks away. A tingling sensation fills his chest. "When do you leave for your trip?"

Near the front door, she stops. "In two weeks."

"It will take me a few days to get some information, ask a few questions. I'll contact my friend tomorrow. That's the guy who can help with your security issue. However, if between now and then you have any problems," he hands her a business card, "call me. That's my direct line."

"Thank you, Julian," she says as she slips it into her back pocket.

He pulls open the front door, turning back to Chandra. "I'm a phone call away. We'll talk soon."

Locking the front door, she moves to the window, watching him as he gets into his car. When he looks up, their eyes meet. She waves, standing a moment longer as he pulls out of her driveway. Chandra glances around her home. Theo is asleep on the sofa. She's about to go up to her bedroom when her phone pings with an incoming message.

"Where the heck is my phone?" Remembering she left her purse in the entryway, she retrieves it. Opening her messages, her heart stammers. Chandra's feet are rooted to the floor.

You looked at ease tonight. Everyone seemed to enjoy the signing. I can't wait to see you again. Did you like my gift?"

Chandra's breath catches in her throat. Her hands tremble as she grips her phone. Her mind is rushing through snap shots of the evening. Concentrating on the patrons at the bookstore, looking for someone who looked out of place. She remembers the guy at the table, but she can't remember what he looked like.

She takes a deep breath, fighting the urge to call Julian before he gets out of her neighborhood. "It's just a fan. You have to relax," she says out loud trying to convince herself. Plus, if she tells Julian or Adam, they will only think her anxiety is getting the best of her. "I'll just handle it. I can figure this out."

Chapter Eighteen

Late Thursday morning

Chandra sits at her office desk shifting her gaze from one end to the other. She came in prepared to work, but there's something out of place and she can't figure out what it is. She opens her lap top. "Maybe writing will help me figure out what's bothering me."

Staring at her screen, the words won't come. She stands moving to the far wall. Now she has a bigger view of her desk and the window. "What the heck is bothering me?"

She puffs out a breath. "I have to work." Staring at her screen once more, she concentrates on her story. She manages to jot down a few sentences before she glances at the clock. She searches her phone for any missed calls or messages.

She thinks of calling Adam or Jane, and telling them about the gift, but she doesn't want anyone to know. She doesn't want the press getting wind of this. Especially if it turns out to be nothing. Then she will really look like a crazy cat lady.

Frowning, her finger hovers over the call button under Julian's name. She presses the button, then quickly hangs up before the call goes through. "Stop, Chandra." Scrolling through her list of contacts, she finds the front gate.

"Security."

"This is Chandra Willis."

"Hey, this is George. What do you need Ms. Willis?"

She cringes as she figures out a way to ask without giving to many details. "Um, by chance, did you guys see anyone around my mailbox yesterday evening, or my house?"

"I wasn't working yesterday. Let me check the log. Did something happen?"

She pinches the bridge of her nose. "No. Not really. I had a note in my box. There isn't a signature, so I was hoping someone might have seen something."

"There isn't anything in the log. You know, a lot of people know who you are."

Her skin prickles. A burning sensation spreads as if she has just broken out in hives. "What do you mean, know who I am?"

George chuckles into the phone. "You, being a famous author, have a lot of fans in this community. We've even had a few people trying to get through the gates to see you."

Chandra's jaw hangs open. "I didn't know that. You guys never told me any of this."

"There was nothing to tell. We stopped them."

"I think you should've told me people were trying to get in here. My safety is at stake."

"Listen. No one got in. Nothing...."

Chandra cuts him off. "What about the other night? When I told you someone was in my yard? Maybe someone did get in and you didn't know it."

"Ms. Willis, I'm positive no one has entered the community that wasn't supposed to be here."

"Okay. Sure. Thanks." She hangs up. "I can't believe they never told me." Sighing, she places her phone on the desk. "Theo, tell me what to do," she says to the sleeping cat.

He yawns, making no effort to move from his perch at the corner of her desk. He stretches, before curling into a tighter ball and covering his face with his front paws.

Chandra squints at the cat. "How rude," she says as she turns her attention back to her newest chapter. Four paragraphs are all she has managed to write. She peeks over at her phone. She reaches out, yanking her hand back before her fingers can grab it.

The fear of this getting out in the news adds another layer of worry. What little privacy she thought she had living here, is slowly slipping between her fingers. All the media will need is a story about fans trying to get into her neighborhood.

"Ugh, what am I doing?" She runs her fingers through her hair, tugging on the ends. "Sitting here doing nothing isn't going to help." Standing and stretching, she decides she needs to get a security company out here. The last thing she wants to do is call the guard gate again.

As she turns to leave, she quickly looks at her desk. The picture of her mother is on the wrong side. She frowns, picking it up. "How did this get here?" She shakes her head. "I must be going insane." She puts the frame back in the spot she normally keeps it. Heading towards the door, she looks back over her shoulder. "Hmm," she says, shrugging. "I must have moved it when I cleaned my desk last time."

She heads to the kitchen for something to drink. Her stomach growls. "Food is always distracting. And soothing."

Opening the fridge, she grabs the Chinese takeout and dishes up a little of everything, leaving enough for dinner. "I really need to go to the store," she says placing the cartons of food back in the fridge and removing a bottle of water. Checking her watch as the microwave time ticks down, her head bobs from side to side. "It's eleven now, if I leave in an hour, I can get my shopping done before traffic gets bad." A task she hates, now even more with the thought of people recognizing her.

Balancing the water and her plate in one hand, she gets a fork from the drawer, placing everything on the table. Before sitting, she grabs a pad and pen from the counter.

Theo waddles in, sniffing the air. Jumping up on the table, he sits directly across from her plate. His nose twitches as he ogles her.

Chandra shakes her head. "You come running at the first sign of food, don't you?"

He reaches his paw out, touching the edge of the plate.

She wiggles her finger at him. "Don't even think about it." She eyeballs him as she continues eating and making out her shopping list.

Theo looks up with sad, droopy eyes.

"That's pathetic," she says. "Here." She places a few morsels in front of him. Watching as he wolfs it down. "You're going to get fat."

Theo scowls, huffing at her remark, while glancing between her and the plate of food.

Laughing, she gives him a few more pieces before finishing it off. As she's loading the dishwasher, her security phone on the wall rings. "Hello?"

"Ms. Willis? This is George from the front gate."

"Yes George, what can I do for you?"

"I have a security company here. The driver said Lieutenant Drake sent him."

Chandra's mouth twitches. She bites her bottom lip, resisting the urge to smile. "Okay, send them in."

"Will do."

"Oh, George?"

"Yes, Ms. Willis?"

"Can you put Lieutenant Drake down on my list of approved visitors?"

"I can. He's a regular visitor out here."

Chandra tilts her head. "I don't understand. Why is he a regular visitor?"

"One of his divisions covers this entire area. When we have any trouble, if it isn't his men, he usually responds to the call."

"Okay. Thanks." She hangs up the phone. "Why wouldn't he tell me he comes out here regularly?" She pulls her phone from her jeans pocket.

"Lieutenant Drake."

"Hey Julian, it's Chandra."

"Chandra. Hi."

"Did you call a security company for me?"

"Crap. I did. Is he there?"

Chandra chuckles. "Yes. He should be driving up any minute."

"I'm sorry. I got really busy and forgot to call you after I set it up this morning. He's going to put in a system for you. It won't be expensive. Chad is a buddy of mine. I'll come over later and check on you. Say around six?"

"I look forward to seeing you. Thanks again for your help." Chandra looks over her shoulder towards the sound of her doorbell. "Hey, he's at my door. I'll text you when he's done."

"Okay. We'll talk later."

Sticking the phone back in her back pocket, she answers the door. "Hey. Are you Chad?"

"Yeah. Chad Richardson." He points in the direction of his van. "Richardson Security. Julian Drake asked me to come over."

She pulls open the door, waving him through. "Yes. I just spoke with him."

"He informed me you're having some trouble. Says someone is harassing you and may have gotten into your home." Chad pulls out a card from his tool bag. "This is the system I think will work best for you." He hands her the card, moving to stand next to her. "I want to install flood lights with motion sensors, on all the corners of the house."

He points to another picture on the card. "The next thing I want to install are motion cameras. When triggered, they will automatically record. Those recordings will stay on the system for ninety days." Chad steps off to the side. "You doing okay so far?"

Chandra's nervous laugh echoes in the quiet room. "So far? How much more is there?"

Chad touches her shoulder. "One more thing. On the front door, windows, and mudroom entry point, along with the side door in the garage, I'm going to install some alarms. If those are triggered, they will alert the front gate. Bringing you help, immediately."

She nods. "I like it. How much is all this?"

Chad smirks. "Five grand." He waits a beat. He laughs at her wide-eyed expression. "Just kidding. Two thousand for the system. I'm installing it for free."

"I don't think I can let you install it for free." Chandra's heart quickens. Moisture skims the palms of her hands. She wipes them on her jeans as she glances around her home.

"No worries. I owe the Lieutenant a favor. This is how I'm paying him back." Chad pulls out a tablet from his bag and begins punching in some information. "I'll need to go in and out several times as I install the system. I have another worker with me in the van. He'll be helping me."

Chandra sticks her hands in her pockets. "Fantastic. I'll be in my office. I'll keep my cat with me. I don't want him to get out." She points down the end of the hall. "Let me know when you need in there, and I will move."

"Great. We'll do that room last. You'll hear some noise as we go up in the attic."

"You can get up there through the garage. My vehicle isn't in the way. Do what you need." Chandra scoops up Theo, who has come out to investigate the visitor. "Knock on the door if you need me."

"Thanks, Ms. Willis." He points to the kitchen. "Is the garage through there?"

She nods. "Yeah, off the kitchen is a mudroom. And please call me Chandra."

Chad smiles. "No problem, Chandra."

She snaps her fingers. "One more thing, about how long will this take? I'm not rushing you; I'm just curious."

Chad shrugs. "A few hours. Providing we don't run into any snags."

She nods. "Okay. Take your time. I don't have any plans." She walks back to her office. Stepping inside, she closes the door. Placing Theo on the desk, she sags into her chair. Her teary eyes sting as she squeezes them tight. "Get a grip." She wipes her face, then stares down at her moist palms.

"It's just a security system." But it's really more than that if she's being honest. Before she signed with Baker and Son, she liked her life. Now it's completely different. She lifts the picture of her mother. "Mom, I don't want to do this anymore." Squeezing her eyes shut. "If you were here, you'd tell me what to do."

A noise from the attic above brings her back to the present. Placing the picture on her desk, she walks into the attached bathroom. Built as a junior master suite, the bathroom came in handy when she got into one of her writing marathons. Using warm water to rinse her face, she pats it dry.

She squints at herself in the mirror. Her pale skin accentuates the dark circles under her eyes. "I'm beginning to look like the walking dead." Twisting her face from side to side, she can see the crow's feet taking roost. Chandra's arms hang limp. Her heavy stomach makes her want to curl up on the little sofa in her office and sleep the day away.

Opening her current manuscript, she dives into the story. Theo is perched at the end of her desk. His purring and the clacking of her keyboard lift the weight off her shoulders. As she types, glancing at the outline of her story, the words pour out of her, filling the pages.

Each tap of the keyboard takes her further away from her worries, releasing her anxiety. Blocking out the noise from Chad and his helper, she concentrates on her manuscript. She smiles inwardly as she writes a scene with her main character. Her female protagonist is fighting against a demon force trying to steal her soul. A battle of good versus evil. The ironic moment is not lost on her.

Early evening Thursday

Tapping on the office door startles Chandra. Lurching back in her seat, she sighs, giggling at herself. "Come in."

"We're ready to do this room," Chad says.

She looks at the clock on the wall. Shaking her head, she blinks several times. She looks at her watch. "Wow, I didn't realize it was this late."

Chad smiles. "We had a few wiring issues to fix."

"Is there any problem?"

"No. Not at all." He motions to her computer. "You were caught up in your writing, huh?"

Chandra leans back. "How did you know I was a writer?"

Chad chuckles. "Julian told me. I didn't know it was you."

She cocks her head to the side. "What do you mean, you didn't know it was me?"

"When he said writer, I just thought like a blogger or newspaper writer. I had no idea I would be putting in a security system for Chandra Willis, horror queen."

Chandra wishes she never agreed to this. She wants him to go away. She crosses her arms. "I don't want you telling anyone about this. I don't want people knowing I'm having any trouble, and I don't want them knowing where I live."

Chad blinks his eyes. "Oh, I would never do that. Not at all. I keep all of my client's information confidential. Please don't worry about that. I'm sorry if I made you nervous." He looks at his shoes. "I'm just a fan of your books."

An instant wave of guilt washes over her. "I didn't mean to imply anything."

An awkward silence lingers between them.

She smiles at him. "I guess this is the last room, correct?"

"Yes, ma'am."

After saving her work and closing her laptop, she grabs Theo.

"Did you get a lot written?" Chad asks as he places a small box on the desk.

"I did. I'm near the end of my current project." She moves to the door. "I'll be in the living room. Take your time."

He nods, turning to the window. "Will do."

Walking to the room down the hall, Chandra places Theo on the bed. Closing the door as she leaves, she mulls over her shopping options as she walks into the kitchen. "I would hit the five o'clock traffic if I go to the store now," she says searching her pantry for a quick snack.

She doesn't want to be in the middle of dinner and Chad need to speak with her. Needing something, she settles on an unopened package of peanut butter crackers. "I hope this is still good," she says sniffing the package. Taking a bite, she shrugs. "Not bad. Not great, but it will help. Filling a glass of water, she sits at her kitchen table.

She feels guilty for how she made Chad feel. Chandra grabs one of the hard cover books from a box in her garage, signs it and sets it next to her on the table, continuing to eat her snack.

Chad's worker is on the porch. She watches as he adjusts the motion camera. Every few minutes he looks over his shoulder, then adjusts it again. Her phone rings. Pulling it from her back pocket, she mindlessly answers it. "Hello?"

No sound.

"Hello? Who is this?"

"How are you doing, Chandra?"

Her hand trembles as she glances at the phone screen. "Who is this?"

"Did you like my surprise?"

"How did you get in my neighborhood?" Chandra stands, moving to the glass door. She searches her backyard. Moving to the living room, she steps to the bay window. Peeking out from the edge of the blinds, she scans the street.

"It doesn't matter how. I can get in any time I want to. Even with your security gate."

Chandra closes her eyes. The voice doesn't sound like Thomas. But she doesn't know for sure. "Why are you doing this?"

"Because I can, and because I'm your fan. I love your books. You think you can hide behind your gated community. But you can't."

"Thomas, I know this is you. I'm not going to let you scare me." She waits for him to speak. When he doesn't say anything, she continues. "I'm going to make sure the lawyers from the publishing house know you're harassing me. I'm sure it won't help your lawsuit. You won't get away with this."

Cackling laughter fills her ears. She squeezes her eyes tight. Starbursts erupt behind her eyelids. "Stop! Stop harassing me!" Hanging up, she slows her breathing.

"Chandra? Are you okay?"

She spins around to find Chad standing in the entryway. Her hand clutches the base of her throat. "Um. Yeah."

"Is that the guy harassing you?" He smiles as he steps closer. "Julian told me about the guy you used to work with."

"Yes." She shakes her head. "I'm pretty sure it's him, Thomas, my former editor. But I can't prove it." She shakes her phone in the air. "He blocks his number."

Chad stands in front of her. "Julian will be able to help," he says reassuring her.

She nods as a flush of heat creeps across her cheeks. "I hope so." She reaches for the book. "Here., I want you to have this."

His eyes widen. "Are you serious?"

She nods. "Yes."

"Chandra, this is fantastic. Thank you." He quickly looks for her signature. "Thank you for signing it."

"You're very welcome."

He places it under his tablet. "We have your system installed. It's a wireless system. I need your password to your WIFI," he holds out the tablet, "type it in here. It won't be saved on this. If you are worried, you can always change it after we leave."

She types in the code, handing it back to him. "Here you go."

He taps something out, then moves next to her. "Let me go through a few things. You can access this system through your phone. As well as the screen in your mudroom, and the screen at the front door. Since you will more than likely enter and leave through your garage, let's use that keypad. Let me show you."

At the mudroom he points to a small eight by ten-inch screen. "This interface will look the same on your phone. After I show you this, I'll help you download it and run through it on your cell."

Typing on the screen, he looks at her. "Whenever you arm this, and I would suggest, you leave it armed at all times. Tap this button and punch in your code," he fiddles with his tablet. "Type in a four-digit number." He nods towards the wall unit.

Chandra types in a code. "Okay."

Chad points to the system. "Now, to arm, press the star button and enter your code. It will beep twice. Go ahead."

Chandra does as he instructs. A loud beep sounds.

"If it doesn't work, press the pound key and redo it. Now your system is armed. You see the green blinking circle around the solid green house?

She nods.

"Any time a door or window is opened an alarm will sound." He opens the door to the garage. An ear-piercing alarm goes off. "Sorry," he says, as she yelps. "I should have warned you." He pushes the star button. "To shut it off, push this button. Now let's say you're having a party. You want to keep the alarm on the windows, but not your sliding doors or the front door."

He points to the screen. "Hit the party button, from there you can tap any entry point you want to take off the system. At the end of your party, follow the same steps and re-engage them." He looks at her. "Any questions?"

She shakes her head. "Not yet." She rocks on the heels of her feet. "Well, actually yes. How do I arm the system and then leave without the alarm going off?"

"I'm about to show you. Say you're about to leave for work, you don't need to take the entire house off-line, just the door you're going out." He taps the screen. "I have listed all your points of entry. As you're about to walk out, tap the home button and tap work mode." He points to the screen. "Go ahead."

Chandra taps the buttons. The light on the unit beeps at three-second intervals, flashing red at the same time.

"You have as long as you need to exit. Once you exit through this door, and you drive out and close the garage, then use your app to arm the alarm. Let me show you. Do you have your phone?"

She pulls it from her pocket. "Here."

He raises an eyebrow at her as he slides it open. "You should have a passcode on this. Or better yet, your fingerprint."

She shrugs, nodding. "I know. I keep meaning to put a lock on there." She watches as he downloads and installs the security app.

"Okay, so here is the app. You're in your car and you just shut the garage door. Open the app. It asks for your code. Go ahead and punch that in."

Chandra does so.

"You see the lighted ring around the house is blinking red. And the house is solid red." He points to her phone as he holds it out for her to see.

She nods.

"That means your alarm is not armed. To arm it, tap the home button. And it will turn on the alarm. This is what it looks like when your house is armed."

Chandra is looking at a solid green house with a blinking green circle around it.

"That's it," Chad says.

Chad points to the wall unit. "You see here the same green house."

She smiles at him. "Wow. That's cool."

He smirks, winking. "I agree."

"If someone opens my garage door, what will happen?"

"If someone breaks in through there, the alarm will not sound. The minute they break into the home via this door, or if they enter through the side door into the garage, then it will go off."

He sighs. "For a long time, I had this system set up where someone could arm their garage door. The problem is, if you enter the home you have fifteen seconds to turn off the alarm. It usually takes people longer to do that when driving into the garage. If it's a kid using the keypad, he may not even have the app. There were a lot of false alarms."

"That makes sense." Chandra says, nodding.

"When you park your car and enter through here or your front door, punch in your code. Remember, you have fifteen seconds or the alarm will sound. Since people don't always move with great urgency to turn off their alarm, there is a fifteen second delay before the guard shack, or police if you have that enabled, are notified.

"Okay, let's say you're out, and someone enters your home, the alarm would sound at your home and through the app. It will automatically open with a diagram of your home, showing you the entry point. The guard gate is programmed in. Having the police notified will cost a subscription. I have included that information if you want to set that up."

"Only the security guards will be notified? And, only after the extra fifteen second delay?" Chandra asks.

"Correct. Any questions?"

Chandra blows out a long breath. "I—I don't think so. How about if I run through the process with you? Make sure I'm doing it right?"

"Let's do it."

Chandra watches from the window as Chad leaves. She holds her breath before exhaling. Verbalizing the pros and cons of her new security system, the pros should outweigh the cons, but it doesn't feel that way to her.

Her anxiety level should be going down. Instead, she feels as if she is about to crawl out of her skin. She can't figure out how she will prove Thomas is bothering her, and she can't imagine who is leaving her presents. Especially after what George said about people trying to get into the community. Going to the spare bedroom, she opens the door. Theo is asleep on the bed.

Leaving the door open, she heads to the kitchen. "Damn," she says glancing at the clock on the wall. "I don't want to go to the store now." Sighing as she opens the refrigerator door for the rest of her Chinese food, she jumps when her doorbell rings.

Chapter Twenty

Chandra glances out the slim window next to the front door. The corners of her mouth push her cheeks up. She bites her lower lip before exhaling. "Hi," she says stepping back from the doorway. "How was..." she screams placing her hands over her ears. "Sorry!" She taps the security pad.

Julian watches her as she inputs her code.

Her eyes are wide when she finally gets the alarm to shut off. "I forgot about the alarm." She's panting. "Fifteen seconds sure isn't a lot of time."

"Hi, yourself. And I may be deaf for a few hours." Julian enters. He touches her arm, grazing her skin with his fingers. He chuckles at her frown. "I'm kidding. How did the installation go?" His eyes narrow into slits. "I see Chad got the system up and running."

Her head bobs up and down. "He finished about thirty or forty minutes ago." Panting, trying to catch her breath, she closes the door. Turning around, Julian is inches from her, his emerald green eyes burrowing through her. She tilts her head down, shielding her inner thoughts. She steps off to the side, hoping the distance will keep him from hearing the thud of her heart against her chest.

Julian follows her into the living room. Her jeans hug her in the right places. He smiles wistfully as his fingers tighten around the key fob in his pocket. "I hope he went through how it works."

She turns to him as they enter the kitchen. "He did. I forgot to disengage it before I let you in. I'm sure it won't be the last time and I'm sure I'll have to call him to ask more questions." Stuffing her hands into the front pocket of her jeans, her body rocks on the balls of her feet. "I want to thank you for doing this for me. He didn't charge me for the installation. Said he owed you a favor."

Julian takes a step closer. Reaching out, he caresses her cheek with the back of his fingers. "I want you to feel safe. If this helps, it's worth it."

She resists the urge to lean into his hand. "Thank you." She glances around. "I have left over Chinese food." She sighs. "I need to go to the store. I keep putting it off. I bet there is enough for us to share. Are you hungry?"

Julian smiles at her. "How about if we get something to eat and then go shopping? I can keep you company and make sure you set your alarm correctly."

"I feel bad asking you to go grocery shopping with me. Seems like a chore instead of something fun."

"I need a few things and I hate shopping by myself. Consider it a favor to me."

"You must like racking up favors from people. I bet it's because you want to be able to cash in on them later. Isn't it?" Chandra steps to her purse on the counter. She pulls out her slim wallet and places it in her back pocket.

"I do kind of like having favors to cash in. I'm not going to lie."

"Hmm. Not sure I like owing you something."

He moves next to her. "You should never owe someone. It will always cost you more than you anticipated." He winks at her. "Are you ready? We can take my vehicle."

Chandra runs her fingers through her hair. "Sure." Clearing her throat, she swallows as she tugs her clothes into place. "Let's go out the front door."

Julian watches as she sets the alarm.

She locks the front door, using the app on her phone to engage the system.

"Quick learner," he says as they head to his car.

Stuffing her keys into the front pocket of her jeans. "I'm sure I will forget something next time."

Julian opens her door, and holds her hand as she climbs inside.

"I'm not a little old lady."

"I'm a gentleman, none the less."

She quickly glances at her phone to double check that she set the alarm. Sticking it in her back pocket before Julian gets into the car.

At the gate he rolls down his window. "Hey, George."

"Lieutenant Drake." He leans around Julian. "Hi, Ms. Willis. Did you get your security system installed?"

"Yes, I did, George. Do I need to give you any information?"

"I'll get the particulars later. There is no hurry," George says.

"We shouldn't be gone too long." She smiles and waves as they pull out of the gate. Frowning at Julian, she crosses her arms. "Why didn't you tell me you work out here?"

"I didn't think it was important." He drives out onto the main thoroughfare. "What are you hungry for?"

"Not Chinese. Something simple, easy and quick."

"Then I have the perfect place." As Julian drives, he gives his passenger a sideways glance. The soft curvature of her face has him unable to keep his full attention on the road.

"Where?"

"You don't need to know. You have to trust me." He flashes her a big grin.

"Just because you're a detective doesn't mean you gain my trust right out. You still have to work for it."

He chuckles. "And what do I need to do to gain your trust?"

"Start by telling me why you didn't mention you're in my area regularly."

He laughs, driving onto the frontage road. "I really didn't think about it. It's not something I readily share. I cover most of the city. This area is part of what my unit is in charge of. It's just my job."

Her eyes narrow as she wags her finger. "I think you're hiding something."

Chapter Twenty-One

"What am I hiding?" he asks without looking at her. He turns onto a dark neighborhood road.

"I'm not sure. Something." Chandra scans the area outside her window. "Where are we going? This doesn't look like a place where a restaurant would be."

"Again, you're making a judgment off what you see. With no other consideration."

"You really like this, don't you?"

He barks out a laugh. "Like what?"

She waves her hand between them. "This... this aloofness. You think you're pretty special, don't you?"

"Uh, you really need to get a grip, you know that?" Julian feigns pain when she smacks his arm. She's about to say something when he watches her eyes light up.

"Wow. I've never seen this place. How could I not know it exists?"

"The owner is a friend of mine. He doesn't advertise, it's all word of mouth. And trust me, he has more business than he knows what to do with." Julian parks in front of a giant Weeping Willow tree. A house that looks like it should be on a plantation in Tennessee looms in front of them.

The building is set back behind the tree. Hanging glass jars with soft glowing bulbs light the porch. Rockers line the covered area. The crisp white of the house and the bright yellow wooden shutters seem oddly in place in the heart of Maine.

Chandra's jaw hangs open. "That's a Weeping Willow. I didn't think they were native to Maine. And why is there a big farm house in the middle of my town?"

"The top of the tree spans thirty feet easy. It's over twenty-five feet tall." Julian gazes at the tree. "This is a different kind of tree. Look closely at the hanging branches."

Chandra stares out the front window of the car. "What am I—no way?" She gets out of the vehicle and stands under the tree, looking up. A dazzling display of thousands of tiny lights, as small as lightening bugs, line each of the hanging branches. Her mouth opens then forms a giant smile. "These aren't branches at all. They're tiny strands of lights."

"They are. Just wait." Julian leans against the front of his vehicle. "Wait for it."

Chandra looks up at the tree, then back at Julian.

He points. "Look."

She glances up again. This time the lights are growing brighter, turning from a soft yellow to a vibrant orange, then a blood red before going dark again. She gasps at the array of colors. "This is beautiful." She spins under the lights as they begin to increase in color again, this time moving through various shades of yellow. "Amazing."

"Did I mention my friend used to do special effects for movies?"

She tilts her head. "No. Is that why this place is here?" She points to the plantation like structure behind her. "It seems very out of place." She giggles. "And yet it seems perfect."

He gestures towards the porch. "His wife grew up here. He promised her they would move back when he retired from the movie business. He built this place a few years ago. Every season he changes the interior. Sometimes he recreates a movie set, a season, a place. Just about anything he can think of."

She follows him up the grand staircase to the front entrance. "Are you sure we can get seated? The parking lot looks full."

"He always has a table for me." As he pulls open the door, a warm flash of air flows over them.

Chandra gasps as she enters what looks like a fairy tale forest. Pathways of a dirt like substance weave in between mushroom top tables. Unseen wires carry fluttering butterflies and other winged forest creatures as they move throughout the space.

"This looks and feels incredibly real. It's like I've stepped into another world." Chandra can't keep from smiling.

A big man walks out from behind a wall, taking Julian in a bear hug. "Julian. So good to see you." He shifts his stance, facing Chandra. "And who is this lovely creature you brought with you?" He takes her hand in his, kissing the back of it.

"This is Chandra, a new friend of mine. Chandra, meet Big Al," Julian says.

"Nice to meet you." She spins around, looking at the restaurant. "This is an amazing place."

"I'm thrilled you like it. When my wife wanted to move back here, I brought all my special effects with me. I had to get the stuff out of the barn. My wife made that clear on several occasions. Building this place seemed the perfect use."

"Well, I love it. I want one of those trees from outside," Chandra says.

"Give me fifty thousand and I'll build it for you." He grabs two menus. "I hope you're hungry."

Julian nods. "I am. I think Chandra needs to taste your honey muffin rolls."

"I've been eating left over Chinese for several days. Honey muffin rolls sound fantastic."

"Follow me." Al leads the way towards the back of the restaurant.

Chandra follows with Julian behind her. A waterfall comes into view. Stopping to watch at the edge of the manmade pond, she gasps at the small creatures scurrying around the scene. "That's fantastic."

Al stops and steps back with her. Several tables surround the pond and waterfall, leaving enough space for kids and adults to get up close to the structure. "I wanted to make sure my patrons would feel immersed in whatever surroundings I built."

Chandra places her hand on her heart. "You have placed me in the thick of a fairy tale forest. I'm in awe." She points to the squirrels sitting on the edge of the bank, before he ducks into the shadows. "I don't know how you did all this. It's amazing."

Al laughs. "Lots of robotics." He nods to a table closest to the waterfall. "I keep this open most nights for special guests. I hope you enjoy the food." He pulls out Chandra's chair before handing her a menu. As he hands Julian his, he rests his hand on the Lieutenant's shoulder. "Sometime this week, I need to speak with you."

Julian nods. "Anytime, I can make myself available."

"Great. I'll stop by before the evening is over. Bon appetite."

"*Merci beaucoup,*" Chandra responds.

"*La dame parle français,*" Al says as a big smile fills his face.

She pinches her thumb and forefinger together. "*Assez pur me render dagereux.*"

Laughing, Al throws his head back. "I don't need to speak in French to make myself dangerous. My English gets me into enough trouble." He pats Julian on the back. "Enjoy your meal."

Julian frowns. "I wasn't aware you spoke French."

A devilish smile creeps across her face. "Hmm, kind of like I wasn't aware you worked in my neighborhood." Chandra takes a sip of her water, winking at the handsome lieutenant. She sits up straight as she watches Julian's face harden.

"I don't like people keeping secrets from me," he says as he leans across the table reaching for her hand. He takes it in his, squeezing. "You aren't keeping any other secrets from me, are you?"

Chandra glances around the restaurant. Her body stiffens. "I...I was kidding, Julian." As fast as his expression had hardened, she watches it soften. The muscles in his neck cease to bulge, and his grip on her hand loosens. Winking and smiling at her, Chandra can feel her forehead wrinkle.

Julian breaks out in laughter. "Gotcha." He continues to laugh as she throws one of the extra napkins at him.

"I hate you right now." She shakes her head. "I thought you were serious and a little psycho."

"I use that same face on criminals when I'm trying to get them uneasy in order to get a confession from them."

"I can see how it works." She fiddles with her menu. Searching for the perfect meal, her phone vibrates in her pocket.

Over the top of his menu, Julian watches as she checks her messages. Her eyebrows draw together as she bites her bottom lip.

"Who is it?"

She glances up, shaking her head. "Nobody."

"Don't lie to me. I can see you're worried."

She leans into the table. "I've been getting more texts from an unknown number. I'm sure it's Thomas. Well, I was sure."

"What makes you say that?"

"Today, George, the guard, he told me people are always trying to get into the neighborhood to see me. He also said everyone in the community knows who I am. Now I have to wonder if it isn't just Thomas. Plus, someone got in and left the gift in my mailbox."

"What do the texts say?"

She opens the messages on her phone. "Here," she says, handing it to him. "I deleted some of them. Basically, things like I'm going to get you. You can't get away with it."

Julian skims through a few texts. "I have put one of my detectives on Thomas. Asked him to pull everything he could find on him."

Chandra sits up straighter. "You don't think he will know you're doing this?"

"No. We aren't going to question him in person. Simply checking his background."

"Have you found anything yet?" She smiles at the waitress as she sets a basket of honey muffin rolls on the table, along with two glasses of water.

Once the waitress leaves Julian answers her. "It looks like he may have had a few complaints from other women. Doesn't look like it amounted to much. Once they reported it, he seemed to stop."

"This could be a good thing. It could mean this will blow over. Right? After the case with the publishers goes away." She reaches for a muffin. As she takes a bite, she melts into her seat. "This is delicious. I want to take some home with me. Do you think they sell these to go?"

Julian laughs at her reaction. "Yes, they do, and we will get you some for the road."

"I don't think I have ever tasted something this fantastic." She moans. "I can't get enough."

The waitress returns with two glasses of wine and their salads, then disappears again.

She stares at the waterfall. Mesmerized by the animatronics, her mouth drops open when a hawk like creature swoops down and lands on a nearby tree branch. "Is that a real bird?" she asks pointing to the creature.

Julian shakes his head without looking around. "Nope."

"You don't even know what I'm pointing at."

"Don't need to. Everything in here is a prop." He sets his salad plate off to the side. Staring at her, he's enamored by her response as she takes in her surroundings. The expression of joy on her face makes him glad he brought her here. She needed the distraction.

Chandra catches him watching her. "What?"

"What…what?"

"Why are you staring at me?"

"You look happy."

Taking a sip of her wine, she relaxes into her chair, sighing. "I am. I think this is the first time in a long while I haven't been afraid or anxious." She breaks eye contact. "I must sound like a fool."

"Not at all. I'm glad I'm the one who could help you relax."

She squints at him, about to say something, when their food arrives. Her eyes bulge at the massive amount of pasta. "I can make three meals out of this."

"Seeing as how you suck at grocery shopping, that's a good thing."

She frowns. "Ha ha. I don't suck at it; I hate doing it. Big difference."

They eat in silence for a few moments.

Able to enjoy her meal without the added pressure of conversation, is even more blissful. Chandra watches Julian as he eats. His square, rugged jaw line adds to his appealing looks. His dark hair is striking against his emerald green eyes.

"Now I'm the one being watched," he says without looking at her.

"How do you know I'm watching you?"

"I can feel it." He winks at her.

"How long have you been a detective?"

Taking a sip of his wine, he places his fork on his plate. "Three years as a lieutenant. Fifteen years total on the force."

"Why didn't you go into the FBI? You've worked with them, right?"

"Yes. I've worked with them. They wanted me to apply several times. It's not for me."

"Would you like some more wine?" The waitress asks, lifting the bottle in her hand.

"Yes, please," Chandra says as she lifts her glass.

"And you?" the waitress asks Julian.

He shakes his head. "No, thank you."

Before she leaves, Chandra asks for a to-go box, and some muffins, as well.

"I'll take one too, please," Julian says.

"Thank you very much for this." She stares at the waterfall. "What a great distraction. I needed this."

"I'm glad I could help." Taking the boxes and the check from the waitress, he hands one box to Chandra. "Where do you like to shop for groceries?"

"Hannaford. There is one practically right next door to my neighborhood. You don't have to go with me. I can go out tomorrow."

"Like I said earlier, I need a few things. Might as well get it done together. Keep each other company."

Chandra laughs. "Okay." She finishes off her last sip of wine. "I'm ready."

Filling out the credit card receipt, Julian picks up his to go box. "Let's go shopping."

As they leave, Julian stops to whisper something to Al. He nods in response to something Al says.

Chandra watches the exchange. They seem like they're more than acquaintances. As if there is a deeper bond between them. Leading Julian out the door, she glances over her shoulder. "You two seem like you're close."

"We are," he says, opening the passenger door for her. "I kind of look at him as an uncle."

A wisp of sadness creeps over her. "That's nice."

Getting into the driver's seat, Julian cocks his head to the side. "Did I say something wrong?"

"No, not at all."

Julian starts the car, before he backs out, he looks over at her. "I'm always here for you, Chandra. I hope you realize that."

"I do. Still nice to hear, though." She turns towards the window, shielding her face.

Giving her a few moments, he pulls out of the parking lot, heading towards the store in silence. "Do you have a list?"

She looks at him, her brow wrinkles. "A list for what?"

"The grocery store."

"Yes. I mean, no. I made one earlier. I left it at home. Something I do regularly. I usually just wing it."

"You're the dream shopper for the stores."

"Are you insulting me? Cause it sounds like an insult."

Julian drives into the lot, parking close to the front of the store. "If you don't use a list, you tend to buy on impulse. Buying more than you need, and things you may not have otherwise purchased."

Chandra laughs, covering her hand with her mouth.

"What is so funny?" he asks exiting the vehicle.

Walking towards him, she falls in with his step. "You sounded like a dad or something. It struck me as funny. I'm a pretty boring shopper. I tend to get the same things all the time."

A young man walking by turns and looks at Chandra.

She ignores his stare.

Julian grabs a cart. "Can we share one, or do I need my own?"

"One is fine."

She glances around the store. But not really looking at anyone. She hopes no one recognizes her. Not tonight.

"Just because I'm pragmatic, doesn't mean I'm an old fuddy dud."

"You're just a wise old owl."

Julian is about to respond when he sees a young man peeking at them from the edge of an aisle. "I think someone is looking at you," he says leaning down, placing his mouth near her ear.

Chandra nods. "I saw him when we walked in. I was hoping he wouldn't know who I was."

Julian is about to say something when a girl comes up to Chandra.

"You're Chandra Willis, the writer?"

Chandra nods. "I am."

"Can I take a picture with you?" She doesn't wait for a response, before she places her arm around Chandra's shoulders and snaps a photo.

"Um. Okay," Chandra says.

"Thank you." The girl gushes as she runs out of the store.

Within a few moments the young man approaches them.

"I know who you are." He points at Chandra.

She steps a little closer to Julian. "That's great."

"You're that horror writer."

Chandra's brow wrinkles. She looks at Julian then back at the stranger. "Yes I am."

"I'm an author, too."

Chandra wants to run from the store. Her heart is racing. "That's fantastic."

Julian steps in between Chandra and the so-called fan. "We have to go."

"I think your books are great."

"Thank you," Chandra says as Julian pulls her along. She turns to Julian. "I don't want to be here."

"Let's get what we need. And then we'll go. Don't worry. I'm here."

Chapter Twenty-Two

Driving back to Chandra's house, Julian gets a call from one of his detectives.

Chandra listens to the one-sided conversation as she checks her email on her phone. "What's up?" she asks when he hangs up.

"Huh?"

"Your call. Is everything okay?"

Julian looks out his side window.

"Julian? Can you tell me about the call?"

"One of my detectives found something out about Thomas."

Chandra wiggles in her seat, shifting her weight. She clasps her hands in her lap. "Is it bad?"

As Julian pulls up to the gate, an alarm sounds at the same time the security app on Chandra's phone chirps. She clicks on the app.

"What is it?" Julian asks.

"I'm not sure." She lets out a soft gasp. "It says the side door has been opened."

George comes out from the gate. "Hey, Lieutenant Drake." An alarm sounds in the shack. He glances over his shoulder then back at Chandra. "That alarm is from your house," George says nodding towards the shack.

"Let us in," Julian says.

"You got it. Call me if I need to do anything for you," George says.

Chandra uses the app to shut off the alarm.

Julian speeds through the gate. He glances over at Chandra. Her eyes are glossy from the tears welling up. "Don't worry." He reaches over and takes her hand.

She looks at him. She can't keep the salty tears from cresting over the edge. She grips his hand tight, saying nothing as he drives to her house.

Entering the driveway, nothing looks out of place. Julian scans the front yard and garage area. He looks over at Chandra. "Stay here. I mean it."

Chandra nods. "Okay." She grips her phone in her hand.

"I'll be back to get you." Julian grabs his weapon from the glove box, and jumps out of the car.

Chandra watches as he walks around the garage to the side door. Her knee bounces as she wrings her hands. "C'mon," she whispers as she looks over her shoulder. She checks the locks on the car door, making sure they're secure. The still of the night echoes in her ears. Her teeth chatter as she waits for Julian to return.

Shifting in her seat, she searches the darkness for signs of a would-be assailant. Her thoughts race as she thinks of Theo. She squeezes her eyes shut, rocking in her seat. "Please, please let Theo be okay." She repeats the mantra over and over again.

She hears the click of the door lock. She sinks into the seat, hiding. She sees Julian walking towards her. Opening the door, she leaps from the car. "Is anyone there?"

Julian shakes his head. "No."

"Does it look like they went into the house?"

He takes her by her elbow, walking towards the garage. "Not from what I could see. I think they jimmied it open ran off when the alarm sounded. Did you disarm the home using the app?"

"Yes." Using the keypad to raise the door, she unlocks the mudroom. Her brow furrows as she glances at the side door. "Can it be locked?"

"Sort of."

"That doesn't make me feel safe." Before entering the house, she closes the garage door. Scanning her living room, nothing looks out of place. "Where's Theo?" she asks, frantically searching the living room and the rest of the downstairs. She walks out of the spare bedroom. "Theo? Here kitty, kitty?" Chandra runs to the glass door. Spinning around, she finds Julian right behind her. "Did you see him?"

"No. I wanted to make sure whoever tried to get in didn't actually succeed. The mudroom was still locked so I couldn't get into the house." His gaze lands on her. Tears stream down her face. "We'll find him, I promise. Only the side door was opened. He has to still be in the house."

Chandra races through the house again. Checking upstairs, then a second pass of the downstairs. "Theo? C'mon kitty. It's Mama. Sweetie? Here kitty, kitty." She's about to search the downstairs again, when a soft meow catches her attention.

Following the noise, she finds Theo under the bed in the guest bedroom. "I found him." She calls out to Julian. "I must have missed him the first time I looked under here." Dragging him out, she hugs him against her chest. "Oh, Theo. Are you okay?"

Julian reaches out and scratches his head. "I bet the alarm spooked him."

"I don't doubt it."

"Well, it also looks like it did its job."

"I still don't feel safe. I thought the alarm would make me feel safe." She buries her face in Theo's fur.

Chapter Twenty-Three

Chandra moves around in a daze as she helps put up her groceries. Her eyes dart to the mudroom, then back to her task.

"Don't worry. I'm calling a friend of mine to come over this evening and fix the side door and check all the other locks." Julian grabs a bottle of wine from the fridge and one glass. "Sit." He motions towards a chair at the table.

Theo is oblivious. He eats his food as if nothing has happened.

"Take a cue from the cat and relax. I know this is scary. I promise we'll get the side door fixed." He pulls out his phone and texts someone. A few minutes later it pings. "My friend is on his way. He said he should be here in about thirty minutes."

A faint smile pulls her mouth upward. "Thank you."

"Let's check the video."

She looks at him. Closing her eyes, she rubs her temples. "What video?"

Julian taps her knee. "The video from the alarm system."

Her eyes widen. "I forgot." She pulls her phone from her back pocket and opens the app, handing it to him.

Julian watches as a man in dark clothing comes into view. He sneaks up to the door. Even when the flood light comes on, the man makes no attempt to flee the scene. He holds the phone out. "Does this guy look familiar? I know he is covered up, but does anything stand out to you?"

Chandra takes the phone. She stares at it. She watches him creep around her home then use some kind of tool to break in. She shakes her head. "I don't think so. I haven't seen Thomas in a while, but he doesn't have his build. This guy seems a little thinner. Thomas is beefier."

"Okay." He reaches out squeezing her shoulder. "We will figure it out."

She nods, sipping her wine.

"Do you have any book signings this week or next?" Julian asks sticking his right hand into his front pocket, quickly removing it. He adds a little more wine to her glass. He holds the bottle up. "I bet you have one big glass left." He opens the refrigerator door, peeking over his shoulder at her, before pushing the cork into the bottle and setting in on the shelf.

"I know what you're trying to do."

"Oh, yeah? What's that?"

"Distract me."

Julian sits back at the table. "You think you're so smart, huh?" He winks at her. "Do you have any?"

"Do I have any what?"

"Any book signings?"

She nods. "Yes. One tomorrow, late afternoon, and one Saturday evening. The one Saturday should be the last one before my trip."

Julian tilts his head to the side. "Where is the one tomorrow?"

"It's at a little boutique book store in Bedford."

"I can't be there. I can pick you up and take you to the one on Saturday evening."

Her head swivels back and forth. "No. You're not my babysitter." She sits up a little straighter in her chair. "You were about to tell me something earlier, about Thomas."

"It can wait."

"No. Tell me." Her eyes squint at him. "Please."

He sighs. "It seems Thomas did this to another author many years ago."

"I don't get it. How come it never showed on his record? I know my publishing house would have done a background check."

"It never went to court. We found the records only because we were looking at places he lived. This information wasn't public. I mean, someone would have to know where to look."

"How can he get away with this?"

Julian shrugs. "It's how our justice system is set up. He never did anything overt. Not enough to warrant a TRO or any kind of harassment charges. From what my detective gathered, the young author made several complaints, but never had any proof. The police couldn't do anything without any proof."

"Do you know what happened to the lady? Maybe I could talk to her now." Chandra shifts in her seat.

"I'm sorry. It looks like she died in a car wreck. About a year and a half ago." Julian walks to the fridge to get a bottle of water. "You don't mind, do you?" he holds it up.

"No. Not at all. Please, help yourself." She stares out the glass door. Turning to face him, tears threaten to overflow again. "Do you think he had anything to do with her death?"

Julian sits back down, reaching out for her hand. "I have my guy looking at it more thoroughly. It's looking like a random car accident."

Theo rubs against Julian's leg. He bends over, picking him up. "Hey you." Giving his head a scratch, he places him in his lap.

"He seems to really like you."

Julian grins at her. "I have a way with cats."

The doorbell chimes, making Chandra jump. She stiffens in her seat.

Julian hands her the cat. "It's okay. That's my buddy." As he walks to the front door, he looks back to see Chandra wiping her cheeks. "Hey, Mark."

"Don't forget the alarm..." she trails off. Chandra's brow wrinkles. "I must not have armed it."

Julian smiles at her. "Yeah. Good thing too. I don't' want to lose my hearing." He turns back to Mark. "Thanks for coming over this time of night. I owe you one."

"Don't mention it. You've done a ton of stuff for me." Mark shakes his hand, squeezing his shoulder at the same time. "Explain it to me."

He shows him the side door, while he explains the alarm system. Julian leads him back into the house. "I would like for you to look at the sliding door too and let's make sure the front door is secure, as well," Julian says leading him to the glass doors. "What do you think?"

Mark examines the doors. "These are top notch. Most glass doors ride on a rail system. These have posts in each of the corners of the frames of glass. He turns to Chandra. "This has a remote, correct?"

She lifts it off the little round table, next to a reading chair. "Yes," she says, handing it to him.

Using the remote, he tests the door, opening it and closing it several times. He whistles, watching as the frames of glass fold open like an accordion, then close flat with no visible seams. "These are nice. The metal posts ride on a track that is buried." He opens the door. "See that groove there?" he asks looking at Julian while pointing to the floor. "It gives the illusion the doors are free standing. When the door is shut, the frames inter lock with each other forming a very tight seal. There are two edges that keep a slim tool from being used to pry the glass open."

He takes a few steps to his right, pointing at the floor. "This is the locking mechanism, correct?"

Chandra nods.

He glances at Julian. "When she taps it, it engages the post within the track, essentially locking the underground poles in place." He turns to Chandra. "Do you know what's cool about this door?"

Her eyes get wide. "No. What should I know?"

Mark laughs. "I bet they told you and you've forgotten. The doors will still operate with a power loss."

"Yes!" Chandra exclaims. "I remember that. Something about an independent motor."

"Yeah. It won't last long. But if there is a power outage, you have enough charge to open or close these doors. That way you don't get stuck with them open during a storm." He inspects it. "Everything with this looks great. You got the top of the line with this one. I don't think you have to worry about anyone breaking in through here, unless they break the glass. Did this come with two remotes?"

She nods. "Yes. I have another one in the drawer there." She points to the reading table.

"Good. Don't lose it. They're super expensive to replace." He looks back at the entryway. "Now the side door needs some work."

"Can you make it more secure?" Chandra asks.

"I sure can. I'm going to install a few new dead bolts and a metal panel that will help keep the door from being kicked in. I'll put the same on the front door."

Julian smiles at Chandra. "Mark will make sure no one can get in through any of the doors or windows." He turns to his buddy. "I want you to check everything. Put whatever hardware you need to make it harder for someone to gain entry."

"Not everything is fool proof," Mark says.

"Let's at least make it as hard as possible." Julian takes her hand in his. "I'm going to run my stuff home and grab a change of clothes. I'll sleep in your spare room tonight, to give you a little peace of mind."

"You don't have to." Chandra bites her bottom lip. She takes her glass to the sink. Her hands are sweaty, and the glass nearly slips from her grasp.

"I don't have to do anything. I want to." He spins around to Mark. "How long will you be here?"

He looks at his watch. "I should be done in about an hour, maybe two."

"Good. That puts it at about ten or eleven." Julian places his hands on her shoulders. "Mark will be here, and I'll be back in about an hour."

"Are you sure you don't mind? I feel stupid having you stay."

"I don't mind at all." He spins around to face Mark. "I really appreciate this."

"No problem, Julian. I'm going to go out to my truck and get the things I need. After I do the side door, I'll check everything else."

"Thank you. Go in and out as you need. The alarm is off." She follows Julian to the door. "Thank you."

He caresses her cheek. "You're welcome." Leaning in, he abruptly stops, straightening. "I'll be back soon."

Chapter Twenty-Four

Luke enters his home. From his front window he can see Chandra's house. He probably shouldn't have gone over there, but he couldn't help himself. And although he doesn't think she will put two and two together, he still shouldn't have done it. "I'm so stupid he says," as he smacks the side of his head. "That damn alarm. How could I have forgotten she put that in?" He hisses out a breath as he grinds his teeth.

He watches through his blinds as a locksmith pulls into the driveway. A few moments later the car that drove Chandra home, leaves. "I should've taken a photo of the license plate." He paces his living room. A low rumble fills his chest. "I need to find out if that is a boyfriend or just a friend."

Seeing her around town or at the library just isn't enough anymore. He needs to get her alone. If she would give him a chance, he's positive she would like him. What a trophy she would be, too. He laughs. "The family and my buddies would have to respect me if I showed up with her on my arm."

He still has a few weeks. That should be enough time to weasel himself into her life. He walks to his kitchen and grabs a soda from his fridge. He closes the door and looks at the array of photos he has of her. Some were taken at book signings and some taken while she sat on her back deck. One in particular had her hair blowing across her face. Her pale blue eyes peaked out from behind the strands. Her soft pink lips are parted, as if she waited for a kiss. He closes his eyes and imagines what it would feel like to kiss her.

After reading her books, and following her career, he feels as if he knows her. He knows her favorite color is pink. And he recently found out roses were her favorite flower. He has some ideas he thinks will help him get into her good graces.

He fiddles with his phone. Looking at the most recent photo he took of her. She really is a beautiful woman. He should've gone into the library, but he didn't want to risk the chance of her seeing him. The desire to be near her sometimes gets the best of him.

Finishing his soda, he checks his watch. He needs to be at a meeting in the morning, but he has to make one stop on his way out. Then his afternoon will be free, and he hopes he can see her. He knows where her next book signing is. Maybe he should swing by. He wouldn't mind having a signed copy of her book.

Chapter Twenty-Five

10:30 p.m. Thursday night

Mark walks into the living room. He stops and watches as Chandra dozes on the sofa. Her TV is on, and the news is getting ready to start. "Ms. Willis?" He calls out to her. Moving closer, he places his hand on her shoulder. "Ms....."

Chandra screams.

"I'm sorry," Mark's hands are raised. "I called your name several times."

The doorbell rings. "It's okay," she says catching her breath. Jumping up from the sofa, she heads to the front door. Relief washes over her when she opens it to find Julian standing there.

"Are you all right?"

"I scared the crap out of her." Mark is holding his tool box as he walks towards them. "Everything is secure. I placed new locks on the windows. Most could be open by sliding any kind of tool between the frames.

"I don't know if you had any break-ins, but the office window looked as if it had been pried open at one point. I put in new bolts on each door, and two new ones on the side door leading from the yard into the garage, and two new ones on the mudroom door."

"I can't believe I slept through you working." Her eyes shift between Mark and Julian.

"No worries." He hands her several keys. "There are two sets of keys for each lock. I have them labeled." Mark opens up the front door, then turns back. "Leave the key marked #1 in this lock. You can't open it from the outside. Don't lose the keys or you have to get new ones. Lock it when you go to bed or leave the house through the garage. It can't be picked and it will give you a little more protection from someone busting down the door. I put the same lock on the side door. Put the key marked #2 in it. If you need me, you call me."

"Wait, don't I need to pay for all this?"

Mark nods. "I'll mail out a bill. I have all your information. No need to worry about it now. It's late. Goodnight." He waves as he leaves.

"Thanks, Mark. I owe you." Julian locks the front door. "I need the key for the new lock."

Chandra stares at him.

"Chandra?"

"Huh? Oh, sorry." She hands him the key marked #1. "I wasn't paying attention."

He points to the keypad. "Arm your system."

She obeys, punching in the code. "I'll put the other key in the side door tomorrow."

"You go on up to bed. I'll be down here in the spare room."

Chandra nods. "Okay." As she walks away, she stops, turning back towards him. "I feel much safer with you here. I know the locks are in place, and the door is fixed. But I'm glad you're staying." She's about to head to the stairs when her phone rings. Lifting it from the back pocket of her jeans, her hands tremble.

Julian takes a few steps in her direction. "What is it, Chandra?"

"It's a photo."

"Of what?"

"Of me. In front of the library. With a text."

Julian takes her phone from her outstretched hand. He reads the text.

Sorry I missed you.

"I told you about the card at the library. Then that bouquet at my front door."

"What day was that, again?"

"Wednesday. Yesterday."

He scrolls through her call log. "It's from an unknown number."

"Do you think it's Thomas?"

Julian hands her back the phone. "Thomas, or the guy who tried to break in tonight, if they aren't the same person. I'm going to assume it's Thomas. He's trying to terrorize you. This is the same stuff he did to the other girl." He pulls her into him, hugging her. He feels her body tremble against his. "I promise you I won't let him hurt you."

Chandra inhales his masculine smell, soaking up his essence. Something about the aroma brings her comfort. A familiarity. The warmth of his body engulfs her, calming her. Her grip tightens around his waist. "But I took him off the list. How can he get back in?"

"You don't live in Fort Knox, Chandra." He leans back, lifting her chin. "I won't let him hurt you. I'll find a way to stop him."

She steps back, wanting to run to the stairs. "What time do you need to leave in the morning?"

"I'll be out of here by eight or eight thirty."

"Okay. I'll be up before then. Please don't leave without saying anything."

"I won't. I promise."

"Goodnight." She scoops up Theo from the sofa, leaving the kitchen light on. At the top of the stairs she hears the bathroom door close. She contemplates sleeping down here in the living room. Or maybe even with him. But she can't bring herself to ask. Gathering her strength, she heads to her room.

Dressing for bed, she snuggles in her sweats and t-shirt. Theo crawls up next to her. Her bedroom door is cracked, allowing Theo to get out. The glow from the hallway night light casts long shadows into her room.

Her mind races as her breathing comes in short pants. The shadows creep around her room as if they're spying on her, waiting for the right moment to attack. Scenarios run through her mind. How long would it take him to get up here? Would he make it in time? Clenching and unclenching the blankets in her hands, her breathing slows. No longer able to keep her eyes open, they drift shut.

Chapter Twenty-Six

4:30 a.m. Friday morning

A whisper tickles Chandra's ear. She swats at whatever is trying to wake her.

"Chandra." The voice whispers again.

Her eyes pop open. She holds her breath. Squeezing her eyes shut, her body stiffens under the covers.

"Chandra."

She bolts upright. A dark figure stands in her doorway. She can't see his face, yet she senses something familiar about him. She relaxes. "Julian, is that you?"

No response.

The man takes a step towards her.

The hair on her arms bristle. Sweat beads around her hairline. "Julian?"

In a flash, the man leaps to her. Jumping on the bed, he straddles her.

Chandra struggles against his weight. She sees the knife in his hand. The man is wearing a plastic mask, distorting his features. She frees one of her pinned arms and reaches up to pull the mask off. A swoosh of air escapes her lungs as she screams before the knife plunges into her stomach. The last face she sees is Julian's.

"Chandra! Chandra! Wake up!" Julian is holding her arms against the bed. "Chandra! It's okay. It's me."

Chandra wiggles free of his hold.

Julian sits next to her on the bed. He reaches out to push her hair out of her face. "Chandra, it's me, Julian."

She scurries to the other side of the bed, leaping onto the floor. Her eyes are wide, tears stream down her cheeks. "It was you." Her hand grabs her stomach. She checks herself for blood.

"It was me what?" Julian asks as he turns on the overhead light. "Chandra, you were screaming in your sleep."

"It was you." She points at him.

He takes a few steps towards her. "Chandra. You were having a bad dream."

"Stay away. Just stay there." Her legs tremble, barely able to support her. She stumbles.

Julian grabs her; moving her to the end of the bed. "Sit."

She shrinks at the tone in his voice. Wrapping her arms around her waist, she rocks back and forth.

Julian stands in front of her. "Tell me about your dream."

She breathes in through her nose and out through her mouth. It takes several slow breaths to calm herself. She places the thumb of her right hand against each fingertip. Repeating the process until the mental fog leaves.

Julian can hear her counting, one, two, three, four; under her breath. The sequence slowing with each repetition. "Talk to me, Chandra." He sits next to her, placing his arm around her shoulders.

"Someone called my name. I looked up, and a man stood in my doorway. Before I knew it, he jumped on top of me, pinning me down. He wore a mask. I ripped it off as he stabbed me." She lifts her head to look at him. "It was you."

"I don't understand."

"When I removed his mask. It was you. You killed me."

Julian tightens his grip around her, pulling her into the crook of his shoulder. "It was a bad dream." Excess saliva coats his throat. The hair at the nape of his neck stiffens. His grip around her tightens. "It was a bad dream." Sneaking a peak at his watch, he sighs. "It's almost five. I'm going to go take a shower," he says, standing.

Chandra's posture slumps. "I'm sorry. You must think I'm a nut case."

He places a little distance between them. "No. I don't."

"You seem—angry."

His head hangs low. "I'm not angry. I don't know what to do to help you. I know you don't really think I could kill you. I hate seeing you hurting and scared."

She looks up at him. Her bottom lip trembles. She takes one step towards him, stopping. Chandra fidgets with the hem of her shirt. "I know you would never hurt me." She lifts her gaze upward, making eye contact before looking down at her feet. "My subconscious put you in Thomas' place." Stepping next to him, she wraps her arms around his waist. "Thank you for being here."

He kisses the top of her head as he hugs her. "Of course. Where else would I be?" He lifts her chin. "I like being with you. I wish I could make you realize I won't let anyone hurt you."

Chandra lays her head against his chest, inhaling. The soft beating of his heart soothes her. "I know." She steps back. "I know you will protect me."

"I hope you do." His fingers graze her cheek.

She clears her throat. "While you're showering, I'll make you breakfast."

He lifts one eyebrow at her. "What kind of breakfast?"

"A full Irish," she says walking to the door.

He follows behind her. "I could get used to this."

At the bottom of the stairs they part ways. Julian heads to the guest bathroom and Chandra to the kitchen.

Theo is hot on her heels. His meowing echoes around her.

"Yes, I'll feed you first." After filling his bowl with a can of cat food, she washes her hands and begins to prepare breakfast. Something nags her. A niggling deep in her subconscious. It's trying to tell her something. She pushes the uncertainty away. Focusing on the day ahead. A day she hopes she gets to spend with Julian.

Chapter Twenty-Seven

Pushing his plate to the center of the table, Julian washes down his last bite of food. "Best breakfast I've had in a long time."

Chandra beams him a huge smile. "It's the least I can do for you babysitting me."

"And accusing me of murdering you."

"Yes, that too."

"I'm not babysitting you." He stands, stretching. "I like being around you. Plus, you feed me. What man doesn't like to be fed?"

Clearing the plates, Chandra laughs. "I guess the old saying, 'a way to a man's heart is through his stomach', is true."

Standing behind her, he places both hands on the edge of the sink, blocking her in. His lips rest against her left ear. "Are you trying to weave your way into my heart?" He can feel her body shiver, as his lips graze her neck. "Hmm? You haven't answered me?"

Chandra blows out a hot breath of air. Her fingers grip the sides of the counter. Blood rushes to her cheeks, flooding her face with heat. Her chest tightens.

Julian moves his hands to her shoulders, as he presses closer to her. Her lightweight t-shirt hangs loose at the waist. Fighting the urge to run his hands along her stomach, he steps back. When she turns around, her eyes are hooded. Her lips are plump and pink. "I better get going," he says taking two steps back. He looks down, hiding his smirk.

"Okay. Yeah, I have to get ready for my book signing this afternoon. Actually, dinner time is when the event will be happening." She brushes her hair back from her face. Not sure what to do with her hands, she wraps her arms around herself.

"Where is it?"

Chandra feels a pang of sadness as she watches him gather his belongings. She wants him to stay. "It's in Bedford. Frilly's Book Haven. Starts at five."

He chuckles at the name. "That's a funny name for a book store."

She shrugs. "I go where they tell me." She follows him to the front door. "Thank you again for staying."

He turns to her. Inches from her, he can feel her warm breath against his skin. "I didn't mind at all. I'll text you later. Make sure to arm everything when you leave. Tomorrow I'm on call, but I can hang around and drive you to the signing."

"That would be nice." She taps in the code before opening the front door, watching as he heads to his car. He waves as he leaves the driveway. She closes the door and is about to lock it, when someone knocks on it. Opening it she's smiling. "Did you miss me already?" She asks expecting to see Julian. "Oh." The word comes out as a gasp.

"Chandra?"

She takes a step back, placing herself behind her front door. "Yes?"

He smiles at her. "I'm Luke Reynolds." He points to his left. "I live two houses over. I didn't mean to startle you."

"Hi, Luke. What can I do for you?"

"I saw the security company and the locksmith over here. I was about to leave for work and wanted to make sure you're okay. I heard an alarm last night. It didn't stay on for very long. Did you have a break in?" he asks, walking towards her.

She nods. "I'm fine. Making some needed upgrades. Not sure if someone tried to break in or if it was a false alarm." Chandra's mind races. *Where do I know him from?* The silence hangs heavy between them.

"I'm sure having your boyfriend stay over will help."

Chandra shakes her head. "Boyfriend?"

"The car that just left. I saw he stayed the night. I just assumed he was your boyfriend."

"No. A very good friend." She squints. "Have we met before?"

He grins at her. "A couple of times over the last few years. Passing by. I travel a lot, so I'm not home much."

He steps closer to the door. "Did you like the flowers?"

Chandra's body goes rigid. She can barely take in a breath. "How did you know about the flowers?"

He chuckles. "I saw them. They were at your front door. Quite beautiful." He flashes a sly grin. "I bet pink must be your favorite color."

Chandra tries to slow her breathing. "Did you see who put them at my door?"

He shrugs. "Nope. Anyway, if you ever need anything, I'm right next door. Well, two doors over." He nods towards his house. "Don't hesitate to call me." He reaches into the front pocket of his jeans.

Chandra withdraws further into her home.

"Here. This is my number. Call me if you need anything." He hands the piece of paper to her.

"Thank you." She's about to close the door when he puts his arm out to stop it.

"I love your books. I've read every one. The way you capture the terror of your characters makes me feel like I'm right in the thick of it." He tilts his head, making a half salute to her. "I have to leave for work. Remember, I'm always just a phone call away." He glances back at her as he walks to his house.

Chandra closes her door, engaging all the locks and then arming the alarm system. Shivering, she grabs a sweater hanging on the back of one of her chairs. She's positive she has seen Luke before today. Setting her alarm on her phone, she lays down on the sofa. Barely nine a.m. and she can't keep her eyes open. Snuggling in for a short nap, Theo joins her. As she breathes, Theo's scent fills her nose. She places her head next to his and inhales. Drifting off, she can't help but smile. She knows that smell, if only she could place it.

Chapter Twenty-Eight

Chandra finds a spot a few doors down from the bookstore. Several shoppers make their way through the small boutiques lining the street. Checking the time, she has fifteen minutes to set things up. This time Adam wouldn't be here.

Her thoughts drift back to this morning. She can smell Julian's freshly washed body. She can feel his hot breath on her neck. Her fingers graze her phone. She resists the urge to call him. "No. I'll not be desperate. I may be a lot of things. But I'm not desperate." Lifting her purse from the passenger seat and her phone from its cradle, she exits her vehicle.

Shivering slightly against the crisp air, she frowns. She searches the backseat. "Crap. I forgot it again." She sighs, gathering a box of table décor and a second bag. Walking to the bookstore, she freezes mid-stride.

The hair on the back of her neck stands on end. She turns, scanning both sides of the street. Shrugging, she continues. A few steps from the entrance, a tingling sensation spreads throughout her chest. The overwhelming urge to turn around washes over her. She glances over both shoulders. Besides the shoppers, no one stands out to her. Closing her eyes, she stands up straight, squaring her shoulders. "Not today," she says under her breath as she pulls open the door.

The chime sounds and an older woman lifts her head.

Chandra smiles as she maneuvers the box through the doorway. "Hi."

The woman's eyes light up when she recognizes her guest. "Tom! Tom! She's here." Wiping her hands on the sides of her skirt, she rushes over. "Ms. Willis." She places a hand on her chest. "This is exciting. Thank you for coming."

"It's my pleasure." Chandra lifts the box. "Where are you going to have me situated?"

"Where are my manners?" The lady takes the box from her hands. "Let me help you. Follow me." Dodging nooks and crannies in between book shelves, she leads Chandra to the center of the store. Setting the box on a table. "I'm Betty. My husband, Tom, will be here in a second." She stretches her neck, looking for him. "At least I thought he would be."

"Did Adam speak with you?" Chandra asks, placing her bags on the table.

"He did. He sent over all the books needed and some give away promotional items. We're doing a raffle. No cost to anyone, other than signing up for our monthly email."

"That's great." Chandra scans over everything. "It looks like you did all my work."

"I wanted to make sure the set up went smooth. I know you have a few things you need to do, and I wanted to get the bulk…."

"Hey, honey." Tom kisses his wife's cheek. "Sorry. I had to store some things downstairs." He brushes his hands off on his shirt. "I'm Tom. It's a real pleasure to meet you."

Chandra takes his hand. "I'm thrilled to be here."

"Betty, I think people are showing up." Tom smiles at Chandra. "Are you ready?"

Nodding, she places the last of the items from her bag on the table. "Absolutely."

A few hours later, Chandra is clearing the table. *It's always easier to pack up than unpack.* She says to herself.

"Chandra?"

Jumping back, she knocks over a chair.

"Oh my gosh," Betty says, scrambling to catch her before she falls. Grabbing her by the arm, and almost dropping the flowers she held in her other hand. "Are you okay?"

"Whoa," Chandra says with a partial giggle. "Good catch." She nods at the flowers. "Good save, too."

"I didn't mean to startle you." Betty wipes her brow.

Fanning her hand, Chandra waves her off. "It's okay. My fault. Lost in my thoughts I guess." Placing the last of her items in her bag, she arches her back; stretching.

"Your books sold out, every one we had in stock. What a success!" Lifting a bouquet of six different colored shades of roses, she holds them out to her. "And these are for you."

"You shouldn't have bought these for me." She takes the flowers. "They're beautiful."

"I would love to take credit for these, but I can't. They were delivered tonight," Betty says.

Chandra swallows, licking her lips. "Do you know who sent them?"

"No. They were delivered to the back. That is where all deliveries are dropped off."

"By a florist?" Chandra sets the roses on the table.

"I don't really know. A man in a delivery jacket and baseball hat dropped them off. I only knew they were for you because of the card." Betty points to the card nestled between the stems.

"Oh. I wonder who did this?" Chandra fidgets with her hands. "What about what Adam sent over? Did he say he would be picking up those items?"

Betty nods, smiling over her shoulder at her husband. He carries three coffee mugs, each topped with mounds of whip cream. "Yummy," she says, taking a cup.

Tom hands one to Chandra. "I took the liberty of making you one."

"Thank you." She savors the rich warm flavors of cocoa and cinnamon. "Mmm. This hits the spot."

"Who gave you the flowers?" Tom asks.

"Quit being nosy." Betty taps her husband on the forearm.

"It's okay. I bet my agent or editor did it." Chandra sips the hot cocoa.

"Back to Adam," Betty says. "Yes. He made arrangements to pick up anything leftover on his way to work tomorrow morning."

"I hoped you would say that." Chandra sets the cup on the table. "Is there anything I need to help you two with before I go?"

Betty gives Chandra a one-armed hug around her neck. "Nope. We're good. How about you? Do we need to help you carry anything out?"

Chandra shakes her head. "No. I only have these two bags. And these," she says picking up the roses. She places both bags on one shoulder. "I'm going to head out. Stop and get something for dinner on my way home."

"Thank you again." Betty calls out as she waves.

Chandra bristles in the sharp wind. "I have to start remembering to bring my coat." She squeezes the flowers against her with her left arm, as she hurries to her vehicle. Using her right hand, she digs through her purse searching for her keys. Trying to keep it and the other bag from slipping off her shoulder, a noise startles her. She quickens her pace. Glancing over her left shoulder, she doesn't see anyone. She unlocks the car. Placing everything in the backseat except her purse, she then opens the driver's door.

"Who the fuck do you think you are?" Thomas asks as he slams her car door shut.

Chandra screams, leaping back towards the rear of the vehicle. Catching herself against the fender of the car, she drops her keys on the ground. It takes her a moment to recognize Thomas. His dark hoodie covered the top portion of his face. "Thomas, I didn't do anything to you."

"You have caused this whole thing with Baker and Son. I wouldn't be in this mess if you didn't turn me in." Thomas' nostrils flare. He takes a step towards Chandra.

A quick glance over her shoulder shows a deserted street. "You did this to yourself. I'm sorry you got in trouble. It wouldn't have happened if you hadn't tried to ruin my contract." Her eyes widen as Thomas' neck veins pop out.

"Are you fucking crazy? Had you left with me, we'd be rolling in dough." He grabs the sides of his hair, tugging on the ends. "You have cost me everything." He takes two steps towards her, reaching his arms out to grab her.

"I don't think that's a wise decision." Julian steps out from the rear of Chandra's car.

"Who the fuck are you?" Thomas screams at him.

Julian holds up his badge. "I'm Lieutenant Drake."

Thomas glares at Chandra. "You're having the police follow me?" Sweat beads on his forehead.

She shakes her head. "No. I'm not." She looks to Julian for reassurance. "I didn't know he would be here."

"Thomas Rheingold." Julian takes two steps towards him, placing himself between Thomas and Chandra.

"How the hell does he know my name, if you didn't tell them?" Thomas stares down Chandra, ignoring the detective.

"The publishing house notified us. It seems you've been making threatening calls to her. And making calls to others as well," Julian says.

"I have not. I made one call to you, you fucking bitch." Thomas takes a step to his right.

"You've called me several times, using an unknown number. You've sent me texts, and you tried to break into my home." Chandra picks up her keys, taking a step back. Putting more space between her and Thomas.

Thomas shakes his head. His brow wrinkles. "What the hell are you talking about?" he asks flailing his arms.

"You've called threatening me and harassing me. I know it's you." Chandra huffs at him.

"You're fucking delusional." Thomas glares at her.

Julian raises his hands. "That's enough. Thomas, I suggest you leave."

"You've gone too far, Chandra. I'm coming after you with all I have. I'm calling my lawyer and coming after you personally." Thomas turns to leave. "You won't be able to hide behind Baker and Son now." Storming off, Thomas disappears around the corner.

Julian turns to Chandra. "Are you okay?"

Her mouth hangs open. Her eyes dart between the corner and Julian. She points towards the corner. "Why didn't you arrest him?"

"For what? Cursing you out?"

"For attacking me on the street."

Julian pinches the bridge of his nose. "He didn't attack you."

Crossing her arms, she glares at him. "Only because you showed up." Her eyes narrow. "Why were you here, anyway?" She takes a tiny step back.

Julian's head droops. "I came to check on you. I tried to get here before the signing ended."

Chandra takes another step back. "How long were you standing there, spying on me?"

"What? Spying? I wasn't spying on you."

"How long?" Chandra can feel moisture coating her eyes.

"I walked up to the front of the store, realized they were closed, and heard some guy yelling. When I looked around, I saw you. I figured the guy yelling was Thomas. I hid between the cars to listen. I wanted to hear him say something I could use to get a warrant or arrest him. At the minimum I wanted something allowing me to bring him in for questioning."

Chandra takes a wide path around Julian to the driver's door. She spins to face him. "Did you send me flowers tonight?"

"What are you talking about? What flowers?"

"Someone who knew I'd be here, had flowers delivered tonight." She takes a half step back.

"Chandra." Julian's nostrils flare. "I know you're spooked because of Thomas. But, I'm not the bad guy here. I didn't send you any damn flowers."

Standing at her car door, her head falls forward.

Julian rests his hands on his hips. "I care about you. I care what happens to you. How many fucking ways do I have to prove that to you? What can I do to prove it to you?" Julian takes a couple of steps towards her.

Turning around, Chandra stares into his eyes. Their intensity causes a tingling sensation in her stomach. As if a kaleidoscope of butterflies has taken flight. Her rigid stance softens. "You don't have anything to prove. I'm sorry," she says, dipping her head to avoid eye contact.

Julian places his hands on her upper arms. "I would never let him hurt you. I guess if I had let him hit you, I could've arrested him.

However, I couldn't do that." He takes her in his arms. "I'm sorry this is happening."

She wraps her arms around him.

He can feel her shudder against him. He gives her a moment to calm herself. Squeezing her, he steps back. "How did the signing go?"

A faint smile pushes her mouth upward. "It went well." She pokes his chest. "You're trying to distract me again."

He raises one eyebrow. "Is it working?"

She giggles. "Yes. Thank you."

His phone beeps. Glancing at the screen, his face tightens.

"Is everything okay?"

"No. The case I'm on needs my attention."

Chandra squeezes her lips together to keep from laughing, snorting instead.

"Why are you laughing?"

"Your expression. You look like you lost your puppy."

"Hmm. I wanted to follow you home. Visit for a few hours."

"I wanted you to come over, too. Tomorrow?"

A broad smile fills his face. "Yes. How about I pick you up at your home and drive you to your book signing?"

"That's a plan." She reaches out to open her door.

Julian is faster, opening it for her. "I'll call you tomorrow."

Buckling her seat belt, she nods. "Great." She fidgets with her keys. "I'm sorry I reacted the way I did. Thomas caught me off guard. Then when he denied calling me more than once, I—I didn't know what to believe."

Julian rests his hands on the edge of the vehicle's doorway. "It's okay. I would've reacted the same given the circumstances. Remember, he isn't going to admit to doing something that can get him into a lot of trouble."

Her head bobs up and down. "I get that, but I shouldn't have treated you that way. You've been supportive, protective, and kind. And thank you for telling him the publishing house called you. I know you did that to take his attention off me."

He leans in. His mouth hovers close to hers. Winking, he kisses her cheek. "Apology accepted, and you're welcome." He closes her door. "I'll call you tomorrow. Are you going straight home?"

"I need to get something to eat. I don't want to cook anything. I ate the muffins throughout the day. And the leftovers for lunch."

"Okay. Be safe." He waves, heading to his car.

She watches him walk away. A cascade of nausea engulfs her. The butterflies take full flight from her stomach to her chest as the bile hovers at the back of her throat.

Chapter Twenty-Nine

Pulling to the end of the block, Thomas watches the cop and Chandra. He squeezes the steering wheel, making the veins in his forearms bulge. "That bitch. I can't believe her." Staring at the couple, his breathing comes in pants.

"She involved the police. Who the fuck does she think she is? I can't believe she's having me followed." He slaps the steering wheel with the palms of his hands, while rocking back and forth. "She's such a bitch. I'm going to show you, Chandra. You will regret the day you went against me." He isn't going to let her get away with this.

Chapter Thirty

Chandra can't shake the feeling she ruined her relationship with Julian. Waiting for her food at the counter of a sandwich shop, she berates herself under her breath. *Why Chandra? Why are you scaring off the only man to pay attention to you in a long time?* "Thank you," she says picking up her order.

Back in her car, she leans against her seat. "You're stupid. Stupid. Stupid. Stupid." Her shoulders roll forward. She presses the palms of her hands into her eyes. "No crying. I'm such a crybaby."

Driving home, her right thumb taps the tips of all her fingers. The anxiety dissipates with every touch. The rhythmic counting in her head eases the tension in her neck and shoulders, rolling them releases even more.

She has to do what Adam and Julian have said. Look at the events separately. Famous people always get stuff from fans. "Just enjoy the gifts." She says it out loud, but she doesn't believe it. She begins to tap her thumb against her finger tips again. *No. this doesn't feel like fans and gifts. It's not my crazy kicking in either.*

As she nears the gate, George waves her down. "Hey, George."

"Ms. Willis. I've been trying to reach you."

Her brow wrinkles. "I never got a call." She can feel the rush of heat to her face. "Crap." She reaches into her purse. "Damn it. I turned off my cell, and I forgot to turn it on." She frowns at George. "I'm sorry." She turns on her phone.

"Listen. Someone vandalized your home." George watches as the color rushes out of her face.

Her phone pings with missed phone calls, but her security app shows nothing. Chandra's hands shake. "My alarm app never went off." She looks at him with tears welling up. "What did they do?"

"Someone spray painted your garage door." George reaches through the window taking her hand in his. "They didn't do any other damage. We called the police. They're at your home now. I bet your security system caught something, and the app just didn't notify you. The police will look at it with you. I'll be over in a few minutes."

She nods. The jerky movements of her head intensify the sharp pain behind her eyes. "Okay." Clasping the phone in one hand, she drives to her home, her heart beats faster. Unable to slow it down, her breathing saws in and out.

Turning the corner, her home comes into view. Neighbors watch from their yards. Two police cars light up the darkened street with their flashing red and blue lights. She pulls halfway into her drive, parking.

A cop walks towards her. "Are you Chandra Willis?" he asks opening her car door.

Staring forward, tears stream down her cheeks as she reads the message.

You're a bitch and it's time to pay.

Her headlights illuminate the dripping fluorescent green paint.

"Ms. Willis?" the officer asks again.

Turning slowly towards him, she nods. "Yes. I'm Ms. Willis."

"Let me help you out." He extends his hand, waiting for her to unhook her seatbelt. The officer smiles at Chandra. "We took video and pictures of the damage. One of your neighbors has a pressure washer. The paint is still wet. He thinks he can remove it." He leads her over to one of the patrol cars. Opening the front passenger door, he motions to her. "Have a seat. I'll ask you some questions in a few."

Nodding, the lump in her throat makes it impossible for her to speak. She watches as Luke hooks up the sprayer, preparing to clean her garage door. A flash of relief washes over her as the nasty note runs down onto the concrete. With every pass of the sprayer, the letters become less and less visible.

A few moments later and the door is clean. Only a faint outline of the writing remains.

Luke moves towards her, wiping his hands on his sweatshirt. "Hey. Listen, what's left on the door can be covered with paint. I can go out tomorrow and get some from the builder. I can cover up the rest." He touches her hand.

She pulls back. "Thank you for your help. You don't have to get my paint. You have done enough already." Chandra stares at his sweatshirt.

"I don't mind. Let me help you."

"Okay." She nods. "Thank you, Luke."

Luke motions to George. "Can I get the builder's information from you?"

"Sure. Swing by the shack anytime."

The officer kneels down in front of Chandra. "George says you have a security system?"

"I do." She fumbles for her phone.

The officer picks it up off the ground. "Take a moment, Ms. Willis," he says handing it back to her.

Hissing out a breath, she opens her security app to the recordings. "Here." She hands it to him.

Officer DeLeon scrolls through the video. "There doesn't seem to be anything on here."

Chandra's brow furrows. She shakes her head. "I don't understand. How can there be nothing there?

Officer DeLeon shrugs. "I'm not sure. Maybe there was a glitch. Maybe it didn't turn on and record." He gets the attention of another officer. "Check with the shack at the construction area. See if they had any unknown vehicles parked near or at the entrance."

The other officer nods, leaving in his car.

Officer DeLeon holds the phone where Chandra can see the footage. "There's nothing there."

Bile creeps up her throat. Swallowing the caustic fluid, she shakes her head. "I don't understand any of this." Chandra grabs her stomach as if she has been punched in the gut. "I don't think…" her voice trails off.

"What is it, Ms. Willis?" Officer DeLeon's asks.

"I'm not sure. I had a run in with a former co-worker. It could be him who did this. I'm not sure." Chandra's hand goes limp in her lap.

"When did you have the run in with the co-worker?"

She looks at the officer, frowning. She shrugs, glancing at her watch. "I guess around eight-ish. Lieutenant Drake can give you a better time."

The officer flinches back. "Why Lieutenant Drake?"

"He happened to be there when Thomas, that's my former co-worker, cornered me on the street."

"Ms. Willis; can you start from the beginning?" Officer DeLeon asks.

"I had a book signing tonight. It ended around seven thirty, eight p.m. Thomas, that's Thomas Rheingold showed up and threatened me. Lieutenant Drake arrived about the same time. He witnessed Thomas yelling at me."

Officer DeLeon motions to another officer. "Would you put a call in to Lieutenant Drake? See if he's available?"

The officer complies using the radio on his shoulder to call dispatch.

"Where did the event happen?"

Chandra lifts her head. Officer DeLeon's bright blue eyes stare back at her. "In Bedford."

"He would have had enough time to get here."

Officer Riegle walks up. "Lieutenant Drake is unavailable. Dispatch is attempting to locate him."

"Before you leave, would it be possible for one of you to go through the house? Make sure he didn't go inside. Since my alarm or my app didn't work, I would just like to be sure." Chandra asks the officer as she stands. She braces herself against the open door of the vehicle, holding her keys and phone in one hand.

"Absolutely." Officer DeLeon steps back, reaching out to her.

The officer that drove off earlier parks in front of Chandra's house. He walks up to Officer DeLeon. "The guard shack at the construction entrance said only workers and their trucks have been there tonight. They're working in different shifts. But all of them drive trucks or SUVs, and all are accounted for."

Officer DeLeon nods. "Okay. Thanks for checking."

"Ms. Willis, Jeffrey and I will make double rounds tonight. Don't hesitate to call the shack though. For any reason," George says.

"Thank you, George." She watches as he speaks with an officer, then rides off in his golf cart. Walking to her front door, she opens the security app on her phone. "Hmm. That's odd."

"What's odd?"

"My app shows my home is disarmed."

"Maybe that's why there was no alarm or video." The officer smiles at her.

Chandra thinks back to when she left earlier. "I swear I set the alarm."

"Hey don't sweat it. I have a system at my home, and my wife always forgot to set it when we first got it. Did you just have it installed?"

She nods, fighting back the tears.

"There you go. However, be grateful this is all that happened. It could always be worse."

She turns the key in the deadbolt, then turns to Officer DeLeon and snaps her fingers. "I forgot I can't open this door. I have a special lock on it. We'll have to go through the garage." She twists the doorknob, out of habit, as she starts to walk away, when the door swings open. "That's not supposed to be unlocked," she says staring at the door.

"Are you sure you locked it?"

Chandra shakes her head. "I don't know, I'm not sure I did anything now. I guess I could've thought I locked this and set the alarm, but didn't." She places her keys and phone on the entryway table. She checks to make sure the key is in the deadbolt. "Hmm, I have no idea what I was thinking when I left." She turns towards the officer. "Thank you for doing this."

Officer DeLeon smiles at her. "I don't mind at all." He follows her around from room to room.

Theo is close on their heels.

"Too bad he isn't a watch dog." Officer DeLeon kneels to scratch his head.

Chandra smirks. "No. He would be no help if someone got in." When the officer stands, she smiles at him. "Thank you again."

"You're welcome. The other officers checked the perimeter earlier. The outside looked undisturbed. They saw no other damage to the house."

Chandra sighs as she follows him to the front door. "I really appreciate all you've done." Watching as he leaves, the neighbors follow and go home. "Crap," she says when she sees her car. Walking to her vehicle, she quickens her pace, locking the door once inside the car.

Turning the ignition, it doesn't start. "What the hell?" She turns the key again. This time the motor sputters, still not turning over. "What else can go wrong?" She leans her head against the steering wheel. A few tears drip off her chin. Taking a few deep breaths, she removes her foot from the gas and waits a few moments before turning the key one last time.

"Yes," she says as her car engine roars to life. She pulls into the garage, lowering the door before she exits. Gathering all her things, she enters through the mudroom leaving everything on top of a table she uses for folding clothes. Remembering she left the front door unlocked, she rushes into the kitchen. She gasps, stopping abruptly. "Why are you in my house?" Her rigid posture keeps her frozen in place.

Luke is holding Theo in his arms. "I came over to check on you. I saw Theo on the walkway and your front door ajar." He looks over his shoulder towards the driveway. "Noticed you moving your car. I came in to wait." He places Theo on the floor. "I'm sorry if I frightened you."

Her heart races. She keeps a safe distance between her and Luke. "Thank you for catching him. I must have left the door open when I moved my car." She steps to the side, keeping a wide berth as she maneuvers a path to the door.

"No worries."

She squares her shoulders as she passes him.

Luke reaches out taking a hold of her wrist. "I can stay, if you would feel safer." He nods to the sofa. "I don't mind camping out there."

She pulls her wrist from his grasp, stepping to the foyer and the keypad on the wall. "I'll be fine. Thank you again for washing the paint off for me." She pulls open the front door.

"I didn't mind at all. Save you some embarrassment. Wouldn't want everyone knowing you're being harassed. As it is, it will be all over the neighborhood. At least they won't have anything to gawk at."

Chandra bristles. "What makes you think I'm being harassed?"

He shrugs. "I just assumed. I mean I guess it could be someone had the wrong house." He takes a step closer to her. "But I think someone is harassing you. With all your changes and upgrades, it's an easy assumption to make. At the very least, someone is trying to get your attention."

Chandra inches back as his eyes meet hers. The weight of his stare sends her pulse racing. The sound of her heartbeat thrashes in her ears. "I hope it's a prank gone wrong."

"We can always hope." He steps over the threshold. Reaching out he places his palm against the door, stopping it from closing. "I spoke with the builder. He's going to deliver a gallon of paint matching your home. He has it on record. I'll paint your door tomorrow for you."

"You don't have to. I can pay someone or do it myself." Attempting to close the door, he pushes back.

"It's the least I can do." He smiles at her before stepping back. "Make sure to lock your door and engage your system."

She watches through a cracked door as he walks across her lawn to his home. Closing the door, she leans against it. She breathes out through her mouth. Closing her eyes, she tries to calm down. Her body is trembling. She leans against the entry table, balancing herself. She punches in the code on the keypad, arming the house.

She double checks all the locks on the doors and windows, including the sliding glass doors. Using the remote she turns the glass opaque. She closes all the drapes. After two more checks of all the locks, and making sure the alarm is armed, she feels secure.

She places her sandwich in the refrigerator. Instead of eating, she opts for wine. "Julian had it right. There's enough for one big glass." She pours out half, then places the bottle back in the fridge.

Turning on her TV, she listens to the nightly news. Searching for her phone she remembers it's still on the entryway table. Quickly retrieving it, she bundles up in a blanket.

"I need something else." She grabs the TV remote. Scanning the channels, she searches for something light hearted. Finding nothing, she opts for a recording on her DVR, an old Christmas movie. "This should hit the spot." Snuggling in with her cat and wine, she gets comfortable, pushing the fear down.

Chapter Thirty-One

The doorbell rings. Chandra wakes to someone pounding on her door. Theo is purring next to her. "Coming," she yells out. Walking to it, she catches a glimpse of the clock on the mantle. "Who's at my door at three a.m.?"

Through the side window, she can see Julian. Disarming the alarm, she opens it. He stands before her with a bouquet of pink roses. She wipes the sleep out of her eyes. "Why are you here? It's a little late for flowers, isn't it?"

Julian leans forward. "It's nev...." A gurgling noise comes out instead of words.

"Julian?" Chandra steps towards him.

His mouth hangs open. A trickle of blood runs down his chin. "Julian? Are you all right? What's wrong?"

He tries to say something. Opening his mouth wider, blood gushes out. He drops the flowers, shattering the vase on the floor.

Chandra's eyes bulge. She watches as the tip of a blade pokes out through his stomach and slices upwards towards his chest.

She covers her mouth, screaming. She turns to run; her feet won't move. They're glued to the floor. Her skin stretches as she tries to pull them free. Chandra screams jumping back as Julian falls to his knees. Thomas is standing behind him.

"It's time to pay, Chandra." An evil grin spreads across his face. He steps over Julian's body, plunging the knife into her stomach.

She can feel the blade penetrate, as it cuts through tissue and muscle. Blood spews from her mouth. She wheezes, coughing as she gags on the iron taste. She falls to the floor clutching her stomach as her insides spill out. The last sound she hears is Thomas laughing.

Waking up in a sweat, Chandra's head is pounding. Clutching her stomach, she can't catch her breath. She's coughing. Spit is dangling from her chin. "What…." She pants. Dragging her hand across her belly, she searches for a wound.

"What the hell is going on?" She looks at her glass of wine. She doesn't remember drinking it all. She stands. Unable to support her weight, she sinks into the sofa. Her eyes dart around. The clock on the mantle says it's two a.m.

She tries to stand again. Dizziness overtakes her. She flops back down. Black spots float around her head. Bile is creeping its way up. Letting her head hang limp against her chest, she waits for it to pass, taking several deep cleansing breaths.

Feeling a little stronger, she stands. Letting her weight rest on the balls of her feet, she steadies herself. The swaying subsides as she straightens up more. Her phone pings. Unable to bend over and pick it up at the same time, she sits back down on the edge of the sofa.

Her phone pings again. Opening it, she sees there is a message from an unknown number. Her fingers tremble as she taps the glass.

You like being the center of attention, don't you?

She's about to put the phone down when another message comes through.

You have something at your door.

Refusing to let her nightmare or Thomas scare her, she gathers herself. Taking slow steps to the front door, she looks out the little window. She can see a bouquet of pink roses. "No, no, no. This isn't happening."

She takes a few steps towards the living room, before she has to lean against the wall for support. Placing her back against it, her butt slides down to the floor. Her knees are bent, pulled up to her chest. Placing her arms across them, she rests her head.

She swallows the bile hovering at the back of her throat. A cool sheen of sweat beads around her hairline and down her back. Her skin is clammy. Breathing in through her nose and out through her mouth, she pushes the vomit down before she passes out.

Chapter Thirty-Two

Mid-day Saturday

"Chandra?" Julian bangs on the front door. "Chandra? Are you in there?" He puts his face against the small glass window. He can see the edge of the living room. Banging harder on the door, he yells louder. "Chandra!"

She staggers to the door. Yanking it open, her alarm goes off. The siren-like sound echoing through the quiet neighborhood. She quickly shuts it down. "What are you doing here?" she asks, pushing Julian to the side.

"Holy shit. Did you go on a bender?" Julian asks watching her. "What are you looking for?"

"Where are the roses? Did you take them?"

"What roses?"

She closes the door. Setting the alarm, she bolts the door, engaging every lock, before walking to the living room. Chandra falls into the chair by the window. Unable to stop herself, the sobs start. Tears drip from her chin.

Julian glances around the room. It looks like a dungeon of darkness. "What's going on, Chandra?" When he turns back to her, his face softens. "Hey, hey." He pulls the matching chair closer to hers. "Tell me what's going on."

She wipes her face. "Didn't the officers from last night get a hold of you?"

"No. Why would police officers contact me?"

She ran through the events of the evening. "I swear I didn't drink more than one glass of wine. Not even a full glass. I kept having weird dreams. Then I got a text saying there were roses outside my door." She searches her phone. "I—I swear." Her eyes dart around. "There were messages on here."

Julian touches her knee. "I believe you." He sighs. He takes out his phone. "Hey, Steven. I need a favor. Pull the incident report involving 1425 N. Alabaster in Chantilly Estates. It happened last night. Get me everything. Email it. I appreciate it. When you're done, head home. We can be on call out of the office."

"What about the texts? I saw them. They were on my phone."

"There are tons of apps out there to remove text messages after they are read. I'm not an app expert, but I could ask our electronics division. See if they have an idea."

"I was drugged. No way a half glass of wine makes me pass out or feel like I've been hit by a Mac truck." Chandra stands. "I need some water." She picks up her empty glass as she walks to the kitchen.

Julian follows. He opens the fridge, removing the bottle of wine. He removes the cork and sniffs. "Smells like wine." He places it in the trash.

"Shouldn't we test the bottle? I know I was drugged."

"I can't request that. Not without a case. And right now, we have no case. We can't even prove you were drugged." His phone beeps. Checking his email, he reads over the report. "The time line fits. Thomas could definitely be our guy. And his actions in front of me last night, and the vandalism on your property, may open the door for us to question him." He sees her eyes light up. "Only question, Chandra. I can't arrest him."

She takes a long gulp of the water she grabbed from the refrigerator. "At least you can question him." She rinses her face in the sink. After blotting it dry with a towel, she guzzles the last of the water. "Oh man, I needed this."

Julian walks into her mudroom about to check the trash for the flowers, when he sees a bouquet on the table. He lifts the pink flowers from the book store. "Where did you get these?"

Chandra looks at the small bouquet. "Those were delivered to the book store last night."

Julian reads the card. "Looks like your fan is at work again. He must be following your schedule. Does your publisher post your appearances on line?"

Chandra nods. "Yeah. They started that several months ago." She leans in towards him. Her brow draws together. "Why did you go to my garage?"

"I wanted to see if the flowers were placed in your garbage. I'm sure they weren't. That would be too easy."

She barks out a cackle. "I think I'm going crazy. This whole thing is making me nuts." She places a second bottle of cold water against her face before guzzling its contents. "I know someone put something in my wine. And I know flowers were on my porch. I also know I got text messages telling me to look." She glances up at him, her mouth turned downward. "You do believe me, right?"

He pushes a strand of hair out of her face. "I do. Do you have any video from last night?"

Chandra's chin rests against her chest. She shakes her head. "I must have forgotten to turn on the alarm. There isn't any video, and when I unlocked my door, the alarm was disarmed, and the new lock wasn't engaged." Her arms hang limp at her sides. The empty bottle dangling from her fingertips.

Julian moves closer. "It's okay. It's a simple mistake to make."

"But I'm sure I locked and armed the system. I know I did." She wipes her brow. "I feel as if I am losing my mind." She looks at Julian. "Did Thomas do this to the other women?"

"No drugging. There were victims who received flowers and other gifts."

"It has to be Thomas."

"How would he get in?"

"I don't know." Her voice comes out as a high-pitched whine as she pulls on her hair, running her fingers through it. "But it has to be him. I'm sure of it."

The doorbell rings.

"You expecting someone?" Julian asks.

"No."

He follows her to the door.

She peeps out the small window. She leans into him. "It's Luke, the guy who washed the paint off my garage."

"Open the door." He nods towards it.

"Hey, Luke. What can I do for you?"

"Hey Chandra." Luke steps towards the door.

"Hello. I'm Lieutenant Drake. Can I ask you some questions about last night?" Julian smiles at him.

The muscles in Luke's jaw twitch. "What do you need from me?"

"Tell me what you know." Julian walks out into the yard. He nods for Chandra to follow.

Luke stands next to her. "I came home from a late meeting and I saw the vandalism done to her garage door. I called the security gate, who in turn called the police."

"Did you see anyone? A suspicious car? Anything?" Julian asks.

"No. When I drove in last night, I didn't notice anything or anyone. No dog walkers or other cars. I wish I could be of some help."

Chandra squirms under Luke's stare.

Luke hides a snicker. "The builder should be dropping off the paint soon."

"What paint?" Julian shifts his glance from Luke to Chandra.

"Luke called the builder last night to get a gallon of paint to cover the green writing." Chandra stands in front of her garage, tilting her head to the side. The green paint is still visible. A lot less than if it hadn't been washed off.

"Who is going to paint the garage?" Julian asks.

"I am." Luke smiles at the Lieutenant. "I wanted to help Chandra."

Julian raised an eyebrow at him. "How long have you lived here?"

"About four years." Luke's head bobs from side to side. "Yeah, four years."

"Why did you wait until now to speak with Chandra?"

Luke's back stiffens. "Why is when I started speaking to her important, or any of your business?"

"Just getting all the details. Seems someone is harassing her."

"It isn't me." Luke stares at Julian. He smiles at Chandra. "I like her. I wouldn't want to harass her."

"You still didn't answer my question. Why now, years later, did you start talking to Chandra?"

He shrugs. "I found out who she was."

Chandra crosses her arms. "What do you mean by that?"

"I didn't know you were a famous author. When I found out you were one of my niece's favorite writers, I wanted to meet you." Luke winks at her. "I'll still paint your door. I want to help you."

Chandra squints at him. Her pulse races. Her jaw opens slightly as a gasp escapes. "You were at the Book Nook. That's where I saw you." Chandra's pulse beats so fast, her breath hitches in her chest.

Luke lifts his hands. "You got me. I didn't have the nerve to actually talk to you. Let alone get you to sign your book."

Chandra steps back, moving away from Luke. "You made it out like I had only seen you in the neighborhood. Why?"

He shrugs. "I was embarrassed. I didn't have the nerve to talk to you or get your book signed." His mouth twitches at the corners.

Julian steps closer to Chandra. "If I have any more questions, I'll contact you. I appreciate you getting the paint. I'm going to have to ask you to leave the painting until the investigation is over. You can either hold on to it, or drop it off here."

Luke salutes the Lieutenant. "Yes, Sir. I wouldn't want to hinder the investigation. I'll drop it off when I get it." He starts to leave, then turns back. "Is that your car?" he asks the lieutenant.

"It is. Why?"

"Just curious. I thought I saw it here last weekend. At least I think I did."

Julian shakes his head. "Wasn't my car."

Chandra looks from Luke to Julian, then back to Luke. "I wasn't here all last weekend. Didn't get home until late Monday."

Luke shrugs. "Maybe I'm confusing your car with someone else's." He nods at Chandra. "See you later."

Chandra watches him leave. She turns to Julian. "That's really creepy."

Julian shakes his head. "He may be telling the truth. He may have just not had the nerve to speak with you."

"What do you make of him asking you about your car?" Chandra watches Luke as he walks down the street.

"I think he was deflecting. Keeping me from questioning him anymore."

Chandra rubs her arms. She frowns. "Do I really have to wait to paint?" Her mouth turns downward as she stares at the garage.

"No. I just didn't want him around you. I think he's hiding something." Julian takes her by the hand.

"Something made me uncomfortable when I first met him the other night. Now I think it's because I knew I had seen him, I just couldn't place where." Chandra looks down her lane at Luke's house.

"Let's go inside. You need to eat and then shower."

She smacks his arm. "Are you saying I stink?"

He laughs as he shuts the front door. "Arm it."

She does, then places her hands on her hips. "Well?"

He pinches his nose closed as he walks past. "No. Not at all."

"Very funny," she says.

He spins around facing her. "I'm on call today. I'm hoping I won't have to leave. Go shower. I'll rummage for something to fix for," he checks his watch, "brunch."

"Okay. I'll go shower."

He watches her go up the stairs. He tilts his head, listening for the shower. He picks up her phone from the table and swipes the screen. "Chandra, you should have a password on your phone."

Chapter Thirty-Three

Chandra pats her hair dry. The heat from the water still warms her skin. Wiping the mirror with the palm of her hand, she ogles her reflection. Dark circles under her eyes and her pallid skin are a constant reminder of the sleepless nights she's had. The anxiety is crushing and taking a toll on her.

A quick blow dry of her hair, and a little makeup to make her not look like the living dead, she heads to her closet to get dressed. Opting for a nice pair of jeans, knee-high riding boots, and a soft angora sweater. This time she dresses for the cooler weather.

Putting on a pair of simple gold hoop earrings, she sprays herself with some cologne and walks to the bed to put on her boots. She cocks her head to the side. She can hear Julian's muffled voice. Her brow wrinkles. "I wonder who he's speaking with." Chandra fastens her boots, rushing down the stairs.

Julian turns around. "Wow. You clean up nicely."

"Ha, ha." Searching the kitchen, she turns to him. "Who were you talking to? I didn't hear a phone ring."

Julian's eyebrow arches. "Nosy much?"

"It's my house. I can be nosy." She sticks her tongue out.

He steps close to her.

She stiffens at the flash of anger on his face.

He grabs her by her upper arms and pulls her into him. "It's rude to stick your tongue out at someone." He pulls her closer, placing his mouth next to her ear. "It might get you into more trouble than you bargain for." Releasing her, he watches as she stumbles back. He bites his bottom lip to hide his smile.

Chandra's mouth hangs open.

No longer able to keep the laughter in, he snorts. "I got you, again."

Her nostrils flare. "How do you do that? You look angry and—and scary." She trembles, slightly, shaking off the fear.

He gives her a one-armed hug. "You're such an easy mark. I can't help myself."

"What do I need to do to help?" Chandra asks stepping away.

"Grab the orange juice from the fridge, a couple of glasses, and coffee mugs."

"I'm on it." She scoots around the kitchen, fulfilling the list he rattled off. Watching him out of the corner of her eye, she isn't sure if she likes his form of joking.

Julian finishes off the omelets. Getting the toast and bacon, along with a few sausage links, he begins setting everything on the table. "I would've made potatoes, if you had some."

Her voice stammers. "Uh, this is plenty. Let me get the butter for the toast." Opening the fridge, she grabs the cream as well. "Do you want any jam?"

Julian sits. "No. Butter is fine."

Theo jumps into an empty chair, creeping onto the table.

"I see it didn't take you long, Theo." Chandra scratches his head.

Julian breaks up a piece of bacon and half a sausage for the cat, while Chandra gives him a few bites of egg.

Theo purrs as he scarfs down the food.

Taking a sip of her coffee, Chandra adds a touch more cream. "This smells wonderful. And if Theo is any indication, it's going to taste wonderful."

Drinking his orange juice, Julian puts a little hot sauce on his eggs. "You look like you feel better."

"I do. I'm trying to figure out how and when the drugs were put into my wine. It's bothering me. And scaring the hell out of me. But I can't prove it. I only know how I felt this morning."

"You've had that bottle since the charm incident, right?"

Chandra nods. "Yes." She swallows her bite. Her fork drops to the table. "Oh my gosh. Luke."

"Luke, what?" Julian asks.

"She bangs her palm against her forehead. "I'm so stupid."

"I'm not following."

"Luke drugged me."

Julian sets his coffee mug down. "Five seconds ago, you were positive Thomas drugged you or at least had something to do with it. What makes you think Luke did it?"

"He was in my house."

Julian straightens. "When? Why?"

"Yesterday. After everyone left, I had to move my car into the garage. I went out to start it, only it didn't start right away." She points at him. "And now that I'm clear headed, my car doesn't have any problems. It should've started. I bet he caused that, too."

"Stop." Julian holds up his hands. "Slow down. How did Luke get into your house? And fill me in on the car."

"When I went out to start my car, it wouldn't start. Took about five, maybe eight minutes. After I parked in the garage, I walked into my house to find Luke standing in my kitchen." She took a long gulp of her coffee. "I didn't think of it until now. He had to be the one to do it. It's the only time it could've been drugged.

Julian drinks his coffee and finishes his eggs. "I'm going to call one of my detectives. Have him look into your neighbor."

Chandra picks up the plates. Her hands are shaking.

Julian grabs her wrist. "We now have a good idea what's going on. My educated guess, Luke is your fan, and Thomas is trying to keep you from doing anything with the lawsuit, and enjoys harassing you."

She sets the plates down. "I feel like I'm losing control. I don't know when something is going to happen or what it will be."

"I know this is a lot. Thinking someone is capable of drugging you is scary. Why he would want to makes me wonder what his end game is. I sure as hell don't blame you for feeling vulnerable. But we now have a plan of approach. Don't let Luke in your house at all. If he comes to the door, just don't answer it."

She nods. "I can do that."

"You have the tools in place to protect you. Keep your security system armed. At all times." He touches her hand. "Don't let the fear over take you. Okay?"

"Okay." She picks the plates back up. "You cooked a great meal. Thank you." She places them in the dishwasher. She pushes the fear down as far as it will go, concentrating on her task. She stops loading. "You never did tell me who you were talking to earlier."

Julian frowns. "I didn't?"

"Really?" Her eyes narrow. "Who?"

"I called the front gate, to make sure they don't let anyone in that isn't on your list of visitors and to call before they let any deliveries in. Just in case. But I really wanted to ask George about last night. Get his take on things."

"They probably all think I'm a nut case."

"Do you care what they think?" Julian leans against the counter, crossing his arms.

She sighs. "I'd like to say no, but I do."

"Don't worry about them. You know the truth. I know the truth. Those who love and care for you know the truth. Don't let the others occupy your brain." He looks at his watch.

"Do you have to go?" she asks, wiping down the counter.

"No. I do need to make a few phone calls, though."

"Feel free to use my office."

"Thanks." He looks around the kitchen. "Do you need my help with anything?"

"You cooked. I got the cleanup. Go make your calls."

Chapter Thirty-Four

Chandra snuggles under the cover. Theo is next to her. It's warm and cozy. Her brow wrinkles as something tickles her nose. The smell of woods and pine brings her slowly awake. The bright afternoon sun blinds her. Blinking, she adjusts to the light.

Her head swivels from side to side, her eyes raking over the room. "What's going on?"

Julian sits in a chair, catty-corner to the sofa. "Nothing to worry about."

She checks her watch, then her phone. "I don't understand. What happened?"

"I came out of your office and you were fast asleep. I threw the cover over you and decided to take a small nap myself. For the last forty-five minutes, I've been watching TV." He takes the remote and switches off the flat screen. "Did you sleep well?"

She rubs her arms, stretches, then yawns. "Pretty good."

"You snore."

"I do not."

"Yes. You do." He shrugs. "I can live with a snorer."

Chandra giggles. "Good to know."

"Do you feel better? I mean mentally? Is your anxiety still making you crazy?"

She fiddles with the blanket. "I'm really trying to keep it and my fear in check."

"That's a start. Right?"

She nods. "Yeah. It is." She stretches again. "Did your phone calls go okay?"

"They did. I called the officer from last night. I'm going to have Detective Jones question Thomas."

"Do you have something new?"

"With what I saw last night at the bookstore, and the vandalism, I spoke to my Captain. He gave me the go ahead to interview him."

"When is he going to do it?" Chandra asks.

"My detective is on his way to his house now. I should hear something soon."

"I hope they find something."

"If anyone can get a suspect to come clean, it's Detective Jones. He's one of my best interrogators." Julian reaches out for her hand. "Don't get your hopes up."

"I won't. I'm glad you're at least going to question him." Chandra stands. "My signing starts in," glancing at her watch, "two and half hours." She walks to the kitchen. "Are you still going to drive me?"

"Yes. Would you like to get something to eat first?"

"What did you have in mind?"

"Tell me again where it is," Julian asks.

"Tonight's event is at the Bomber's Bookstore, in Auburn."

"You in the mood for the best ribs and hamburgers in the state of New Hampshire?"

"I could always go for a great burger. Where are we going?" Chandra grabs her purse. She snaps her fingers. Let's go out the garage. I want to make sure I lock the front door this time." She starts to head that way.

"I'll take care of the front door. Make sure your side door is locked."

Julian locks all the dead bolts, then heads to the garage.

As they walk out to his car, Luke is walking past.

He waves, keeping his distance.

"Does he always walk around the neighborhood?" Julian asks.

She shakes her head. "I've never seen him in the years I've lived here. Until these last couple of weeks, I never knew he existed." She taps in the code for the garage door to close.

Julian pulls out of her driveway.

Chandra uses the security app on her phone to make sure she turned on her alarm. "This time it's armed."

Julian is about to speak when her phone pings.

Glancing at the screen, she replies to the text. "Looks like Adam is going to meet me there. He has a tentative itinerary and wants me to look over it before our meeting next week."

"That's probably a good idea. If I get called away, you're going to need someone to bring you home."

"I didn't even think about you being called to work." She groans. "I should've driven."

"No harm, no foul. Especially since Adam is going to meet you there."

She glances out her window. The beautiful scenery rushes past. The bright fall colors pop against the burnt orange sunset. Chandra turns back to Julian. "How's your case going?"

He shrugs. "Like most of my cases. It's still ongoing. My unit has a few homicides still open."

"Do you like being a homicide detective?"

"I do. I like solving puzzles."

She glances around. "What's the name of the restaurant?"

"Auburn Pitts."

"Are we almost there? I'm hungry."

He pulls off the main highway. Stopping at a light, he points through the windshield. "It's up on the right."

Chandra's stomach growls.

"Sounds like I timed it perfectly." Julian pulls into the parking lot. Glancing at the crowd, he frowns. "We should get in and out in time for the signing."

Exiting the vehicle, Chandra walks next to him. "I'm sure we will."

As they enter, the door chimes. Everyone looks up, then goes back to whatever they were doing before.

A waitress walks over to them. "Just you two?"

Julian nods. "Yes."

"Follow me." She escorts them to a booth.

Julian sits facing the door.

Handing them both a menu, she pulls a pad from her apron. "What can I get you to drink?"

"I'll take an ice tea," Chandra says looking over the menu.

"I'll have the same." Julian hands her back the menu. "I know what I want. She may need a few minutes."

"I'll be right back with your drinks." The waitress shuffles to the bar, helping a few customers along the way.

Julian watches as Chandra searches the menu. "Have an idea of what you're getting?"

She nods. "I'm going to get the All-American burger with fries."

"Good choice."

After they place their orders, Chandra watches what seems like regulars interact with the staff. She wishes she had some place like this near her home.

"Why the smile?"

She squints at Julian. "Huh?"

"The smile. What's making you smile?"

She sits back. "This place. The people. It has a good vibe. It'd be nice to have some place like this near me."

He barks out a laugh.

She folds her arms across her chest. "Why are you laughing?"

"I doubt you would go there."

"Whatever. I would, too."

"No, you wouldn't. You would order take out. But you wouldn't go in and sit." He sees a spark of anger. "Don't get mad at me. You know deep down it's true."

She rolls her eyes. "I would still like there to be a place like this near me."

As they eat, a football game plays in the background. The crowd around the bar cheers.

Chandra blows out a long breath. Half of her burger remains. "I can't eat any more."

Julian pushes his plate to the center of the table. "I'm pretty full too. I do love the ribs here."

"I can tell." She says pointing to his dish. "I'm surprised you didn't eat the plate as well."

"Funny. What a hoot you are." He pays the bill and they head to his car. His phone pings.

As she climbs inside, she peers over at him. "Do you have to go?"

He shakes his head. "Not yet. One of my detectives is heading to a scene. He said he would call if he needs me to meet him."

"I'm glad."

"He knows I'm here with you. He won't ask me to leave unless he needs me."

Chandra pulls up the book store on her GPS. "If you pull out and turn right, the book store is about two miles down."

Julian points to the clock on his dash. "You have a good thirty minutes before it starts. Perfect timing, I'd say."

"Very good timing." She tilts her head towards him. "You know, I'd say meeting you was perfect timing too. I can't imagine going through all this without you. I'm forever grateful."

"It's all my pleasure."

Chapter Thirty-Five

Chandra sits at the table signing books. She finds it hard to concentrate watching Julian and Adam laughing in the corner.

"I'm such a big fan." A young lady gushes, standing at the table.

"I'm glad you came out tonight." Chandra starts to sign the lady's book.

"Oh, will you make it out to Tamara? I'm your biggest fan, you know."

Chandra signs the book. "There you go, Tamara, my biggest fan. Have a great evening." She hands her the book.

"Thank you. Thank you." Tamara cradles the book against her chest as she walks away.

Keeping Julian in her line of view, Chandra is distracted by the look on his face.

"Meeting you is the coolest thing." A young boy waits for his book to be signed. When his favorite author doesn't respond, he glances around. "Ms. Willis?"

Chandra smiles at him. "I'm sorry. Tell me your name."

"Joey. Joey Standifer."

"Well, Joey, how old are you?"

"I'm thirteen. I'll be fourteen in three months and eight days."

Hiding her giggle, Chandra takes his book, signs it, then hands it back. She reaches for one of the special addition hardback books on the table. "Since I won't be seeing you on your birthday, here is an early present." She hands the boy the book.

"Are you serious?" he squeals.

"Yes. Happy early birthday."

"This is the best present ever. Thank you, Ms. Willis." Joey takes off running from the table. "Mom, Mom. Look."

Chandra watches as he and his mother walk away. The line is thinning. She looks around to see Julian and Adam walking towards her.

"Hey," Julian says taking the chair next to her.

"I wondered where you had gone." Chandra signs another book. "You look like you're about to tell me something."

"I have to go. Detective Jones called me."

Chandra's eyes light up. She stops signing, turning to Julian. "Did they arrest Thomas?"

"All I know is when he went to his house, Thomas became belligerent and argumentative. That allowed them to handcuff him and search his premises. They found green paint."

"Okay. That's great." She nods at Adam then turns to Julian. "Right?"

"It is. I'll call as soon as I know something," Julian says.

Chandra's brow wrinkles. "Will I see you later?"

"I hope so. If I can get away, I'll text. Otherwise, I can come over tomorrow."

"Okay. Text or call, either way." She stands and hugs him. "Thanks for dinner. I hope you come over later."

Julian kisses her on the cheek. "I'll come by. Even if all I can do is say goodnight." He rushes to the door.

Adam takes the seat vacated by Julian. "So, this is good news. Maybe they can arrest Thomas and stop the harassment."

"That would be the best news." Chandra smiles at a patron. She engages in small talk with a few more fans.

"I hear you had dinner with him," Adam says leaning in close to her.

She smiles and poses for a picture with a young lady. "I did."

"And?"

"And that's all you will get out of me."

Adam twists his watch on his wrist. "This should be over in about an hour." He looks towards the end of the line. "Maybe sooner. Then I can take you home earlier."

Chandra leans into him. "I have to stay here until eight p.m. Even without customers."

"Such a stickler for rules." Adam sips his water.

A small lag in customers gives her a chance to take a break. "Have you heard from Thomas? Or anything having to do with him and the suit?" Chandra sits back in her chair.

"Nothing I'm aware of. I did see the lawyers in Jane's office. But I haven't heard what they spoke about."

"I hope tonight means this whole thing will blow over." Chandra sits up as another fan comes up to the table. Signing a book, she hands it to the man. "Thank you," she says as he walks away.

"Julian told me about everything happening to you. You should have told me and Jane."

"I did. You both told me I was over reacting." Chandra signs another book and poses for a picture. She looks at him. "You guys already think I'm just shy, or anxious. I figured if I pushed it, you would think I was crazy. Heck, even I thought I was crazy."

"We wouldn't have thought that." Adam takes a long drink of his water. "I guess I should've listened more. I'm sorry. You know you're more than an author to me and Jane. We care about you. You shouldn't have had to deal with this alone."

"Thanks for saying that." She smiles at him, patting his hand.

"I emailed you the itinerary. I want you to look at it and make sure it's okay. Not many changes can be made, but there is a little wiggle room."

Chandra sighs. "Yay!" She claps her hands together like a little kid.

Ninety minutes later, Chandra squirms in her seat as Adam drives through her neighborhood gate. She chews on the inside of her cheek. She taps her thumb against her fingers on her right hand. Her counting speed increases as they near the driveway. Studying every inch of the front of her house and yard, nothing looks out of place. She breathes out a long breath of air.

Adam turns to her, taking her hand in his. "It's okay. I'll come in with you. We'll walk through it together. Julian wants me or you to text him." He squeezes her hand. "You ready?"

She nods. "Yes. Thank you for doing this. I know he's questioning Thomas, but I can't help feeling apprehensive."

They walk to the front door. She unlocks it, but the door won't open. "Crap. We have to go through my garage. I forgot I have this new bolt thingy." She punches in the code and uses her security app to shut off the alarm. Unlocking the mudroom, Adam follows her to the kitchen.

"Do you like the new system?" Adam asks.

"I do. I like the new locks as well."

Theo sits in the kitchen, waiting for her to acknowledge him.

She bends down and scratches his head. "Have you been sitting here waiting for me?"

Theo stretches and struts to the sofa. Curling up in a ball, he shuts out the noise.

"So much for that welcome." Chandra walks to the table, placing her purse on it. The glass door is clear. All the blinds are open. Julian opened them while she slept and she forgot to close them before she left. Giving a sidelong glance to Adam, she turns her attention to the back porch.

Adam stands beside her. "I checked all the rooms, both upstairs and downstairs. Nothing looks out of place to me, but I don't live here. I didn't find anyone hiding in the closets."

"Thank you. I appreciate this." Chandra's gaze falls to the floor.

"Not a problem. There isn't anything to unload. You don't have any more signings until we leave." Adam reaches out, wrapping his arm around her shoulders. "Enjoy the next week. Sleep in. Relax. And write. You always have to write, per Jane."

"I'm almost finished with the book. I have a few more chapters."

"Jane will be happy to hear that news. I'll tell her tomorrow." He turns towards the garage. "I'll go out this way." He heads to the mudroom. "Come lock it up behind me and set your alarm."

She walks him to the edge of her garage.

He opens his car door. Turning around, he snaps his fingers. "Text Julian. Let him know you're home. And you need to let Jane know about Thomas ASAP. She will want to tell the lawyers."

"I will. Thanks again, Adam." She waves at him. Stepping back, she hits the garage door opener on the wall, closing the door. She locks the mudroom behind her. Wanting a little snack, she gets the sandwich from the other night out of the refrigerator. Cutting it in half, she wraps the remaining portion, putting it back. Removing a bottle of water at the same time.

Theo is quick to check out what she has on her plate.

"Leave my food alone," she says grabbing a can of his from the cabinet. "I'll give you some of yours. Quit stealing mine." Scooping the contents into his bowl, she washes her hands and heads to the sofa. Turning on the TV, she opens the water bottle. The news of Thomas gives her a little peace of mind. And Luke can't get in. She takes a bite of her sandwich, then quickly texts Julian. Her phone pings.

I might get there in an hour. Is that okay?

A grin fills her face. *Of course. Can't wait to see you and hear about Thomas.* Watching the early edition of the news, she finishes her snack and curls up under the covers. Theo joins her, taking his share out of the middle. "Hog." She squints at him. Giving in to his pouty face, she rubs his belly.

She keeps looking at the glass door. She resists the urge to frost the glass. Instead, she tries to enjoy the view. Something she hasn't done for a long time.

Her lights flicker on and off. She freezes, rooted to her spot on the sofa. She looks all around, double checking behind her. "It's a flicker. Nothing more, Chandra." Picking up her cell phone, she dials the front gate.

"Jeffrey here."

"Hey, it's Chandra Willis."

There is silence on the line.

"Jeffrey, are you still there?"

"Yes. Sorry about that. What do you need?"

"My lights are flickering. Do you have any reports of power surges or anything?" She hears a rumble of thunder off in the distance.

"Construction hit an underground line today. The power company has been working to get it up. Most everyone has power, but there seem to be a few glitches. There are also storms rolling in."

"I just heard the thunder. Nothing to worry about, then. I guess. Thanks."

"Don't hesitate to call me."

She can hear Jeffrey whisper to someone.

"I have to go, Chandra. Remember, don't hesitate to call us."

She frowns as her line goes quiet. "I won't," she says out loud to no one. The weather man repeats what Jeffrey said. A threat of thunderstorms over the next few hours and several rounds of rain over the next four days. "Great. Now I'll be stuck inside for the week."

She takes her plate to the sink. Looking for something sweet, she settles on a few pieces of chocolate from her candy stash. Glancing at her watch, she has at least forty-five minutes before Julian can get there.

Wanting to keep herself busy, she decides to clean, starting with the downstairs bathrooms. Once done, the strong smell of bleach fills the hallway. "I may have gone a little overboard." She walks into the spare bedroom. She dusts the night stand and dresser. Her lights flicker again. Carrying on with her cleaning task, she finds herself humming.

A clap of thunder erupts. She looks out the bedroom window. Lightning flashes in the distance. Her phone pings. Biting her lower lip, she's hoping Julian is telling her he's on his way. As she opens her messages, a second one pops up.

Both are from a private number. Her finger hovers above the messages, threatening to delete both them before she reads them. She sighs as curiosity gets the best of her.

It's time, Chandra.

It looks like your book tour is going to have to wait.

Chandra's heart races. This time she takes a screen shot of the messages. Taking a deep breath, she starts to respond, thinking it's Thomas. Then she remembers he's at the police station. She texts Julian. *Is Thomas still with you?* She taps her foot, waiting. Her phone pings.

We had to let him go. We couldn't hold him. But the DA is going to put something together. Why?

I just got a text from him. At least I think it's him.

I'll be there soon. Don't worry.

Chandra decides to respond to Thomas. *I'm not afraid of you, Thomas. Or whoever you are. The police are on their way.*

They won't get to you in time.

Chandra's hands tremble. She walks out of the bedroom, and the lights go dark. A small yelp fills the hallway. She uses the light on her phone to search for a flashlight in the kitchen. "I know I had one in this drawer." She searches another drawer. Giving up she calls the guard shack.

"Security."

"Hey, it's Chandra Willis. Did the power go out for the whole neighborhood?"

"What are you talking about? The power isn't out."

"Jeffrey said some construction work caused a few power outages. My power is out. I wondered if the construction work is to blame."

"No, Ms. Willis. There haven't been any other outages."

She can hear the ringing of another phone.

"Hang on."

She hears a muffled conversation. She cups her hand over her open ear, listening. The guard's voice sounds jumbled.

"Ms. Willis, it could be a blown fuse. Do you know where your fuse box is?"

"I think it's in my garage."

"Go and flip the switch and see if the power kicks back on. Call me back if it doesn't."

"Thanks." Chandra hangs up. She uses her phone to get to the garage. A roar of thunder startles her. She searches for the fuse box. She stands in the center of her garage trying to figure out where it is. "C'mon, I know it's here." Using the flashlight on her phone, she sees it behind one of her metal shelving units.

Opening it, she flips the switch. Nothing. She flips all the switches on and off. Hoping it would trigger the lights. Frowning, she calls security. This time there is no answer. "Great." She walks back into the kitchen. She shivers rubbing her arms.

She finds no open doors or windows. She stiffens. "Calm down, Chandra. It's just a storm, Julian is on his way." She hears her words, but her body doesn't believe them. Her fingers tremble as she calls the security shack again.

"Security."

"This is Chandra Willis."

"I can't hear you. Can you speak up?"

Chandra steps further into the living room. "This is Chandra. It's not my fuse. Can you help me? Can you come over here?"

Lightning flashes. A crack of thunder booms, rattling the dishes. She jumps, letting out a scream. She yells into the phone. "Jeffrey? George?" She looks at the screen. The call is no longer connected. She starts to move through the living room, heading towards her front door.

A soft meow catches her attention. "Theo?" she whispers. "Theo, where are you?" She hears the kitty meowing. Using the light on her phone, she searches for him. "Kitty, where are you." Another round of thunder rattles the sliding door.

She follows the meowing. Standing at the foot of the stairs, her back is to the glass door. "Theo? Where are you, kitty?" Jumping when her phone rings, she looks at the screen. "Julian," she pants as she answers it.

"Chandra? Are you okay?"

"Julian. The power went out. I think someone is here." Another bolt of lightning flashes. A loud crash of thunder booms. She screams into the phone. "Julian are you almost here?"

"Chandra, it's just a storm. Call security."

"You don't understand. I can't get through to them. You have to get here. It's Thomas. He's here."

"I'm on my way. I should be there in ten minutes. I'll call security."

She can hear Theo meowing. Spinning around, a bolt of lightning illuminates the backyard. Theo is hiding under the chair near the glass door. She gets on her hands and knees and drags him out. "I know storms are scary."

Backing away from the door, she whispers into the phone. "I got Theo. I'm going to get in my car. Julian? Julian?" She yells into the phone. Looking at the screen, she sees the call has been dropped. She scratches Theo's head. She feels something around his neck. It's a collar.

Her heart thuds against her chest. Each beat thrashing in her ears. There's a charm dangling from it. The light from her phone bounces off the silver charm. She gasps. It's the match to the heart left in her mailbox.

Chapter Thirty-Six

"No, this isn't happening." She covers her mouth, stifling a scream. A bolt of lightning brightens the room. Another loud boom of thunder shakes the house. Theo jumps from her arms, hiding in the living room. "Theo? Kitty, come to Mama." Chandra tries to grab him from under a chair. Tears sting her eyes.

Another lightening flash illuminates the back porch. Something catches her attention. When she looks at the door, nothing is there. Reaching under the chair, she's trying to get a hold of Theo.

Thunder booms. She grabs the cat by the neck, dragging him out. Another bolt of lightning flashes. This time the silhouette of a man in a black sweatshirt and dark jeans is at the door. She screams, scaring Theo who hisses and scratches her, jumping from her arms.

Chandra runs towards the front door. She hears the glass doors slide open. She turns to see the man holding the remote for the door as they inch open. He takes a few steps towards her, walking slowly in her direction. "Chaaan-dra. You can't run."

Chandra yanks on the front door. She forgot about the new dead bolt. She reaches for the key to unlock it. "Where is it?" She screams. She searches the bowl on the entry table. She tugs on the handle. "Help me!" She yanks on a door that won't budge. "Help me," she screams, banging her fists against it. In a flash, the air swooshes out of her. "Please," she gasps.

The intruder is pressed against her. He grabs one wrist, bending her arm at an awkward angle. He reaches into his pocket. "I think you want this." He dangles the key in front of her.

She sobs. "No, please, no. How did you get that? Who are you?"

He grabs her other hand. "I've waited for this moment for far too long." He holds both her hands in one of his, as he binds her wrists together.

The hard-plastic ties dig into her. She can feel his leather gloves against her skin. "Please, don't do this." One of his arms tighten around her waist. "How did you get my key, Thomas? Lieutenant Drake is almost here. You won't get away with this." She cries out as he uses his weight to push against her. His grip tightens around her. His other hand grabs her throat. "Please. Please. Stop." She pleads with him.

"I'm not going to stop. And I'm not Thomas," he whispers in her ear.

She swallows the bile inching up her throat. "Luke? Why are you doing this?"

"I've watched you for a long time. You're quite beautiful. But it isn't your looks I'm attracted to."

The air saws in and out of her chest. Her pulse sounds like a freight train between her ears. She screams. "Help! Help me!" She tries to kick her front door.

He laughs. "Go ahead, kick and scream. If it makes you feel better. No one can hear you."

Chandra's sobs choke her. She forces the words out. "I haven't done anything to you. Why? Why are you doing this?"

"Hmm. Because I can. You're not my first. Although you have been the most fun. Using your fear and anxiety to get you worked up, brought the most enjoyment. I push the right buttons; I make you dance."

A familiar smell engulfs her. Her mind races, trying to think where she recognizes the odor from. "Who are you?"

"You'll find out soon enough." He tightens his grip around her waist, pressing her next to him. "Fear smells good on you, Chandra," he says inhaling.

Thunder cracks. Sheets of rain pound against the door. Chandra's mind is spinning. "Please. Please let me go. I won't tell anyone." Tears stream down her face. "Please."

"Chandra, I told you I would never let anyone hurt you. That's my job, after all. To serve and protect."

Her heart sinks into her stomach. "Julian?" She can barely get his name out.

"Ah, yes. It's me." He lets his grip around her neck loosen.

She can't catch her breath. "Why? Why would you do this?"

"It's a thrill." He laughs. He kisses her neck.

She feels sick as his breath warms her skin. Making her shivers intensify. "I don't understand. How did you get into my home? How did you do all those things?" Chandra's sobs increase.

"Being a detective has its perks. Of course, you gave me your code. You punched it in right in front of me. Silly girl." He pulls her closer to his body. "Extra remotes lying around. You were so easy to manipulate. Not to mention the perfect timing of Thomas. That was pure luck."

"You won't get away with this. They will find you all over the house."

"Exactly. Why do you think I got so close to you? My detectives know how fond I am of you. I've told them how special you are."

She shakes her head. "You drugged me? Why? How?"

"That was easy. I drugged the bottle that night when I put it back in the fridge. Just enough."

"Why, Julian? What did I do to you?"

"You didn't do anything." He laughs. "I can't take credit for everything. Luke sent most of the flowers." He pushes himself against her. He can feel her heart pounding.

"I thought we had something. I thought you cared about me."

"I do care about you, a little too much. I let this go on way longer than I usually do." He presses his mouth next to her ear. "We do have something special. I'm positive no other woman will make me feel the way you do. Did." His sinister laugh echoes in the dead quiet home.

He drags her back, spinning her to face the mirror in the entryway, pinning her between him and the table. "Oh, Chandra. You should've paid better attention to your dreams and the little nagging voice telling you to be afraid of me." He watches her in the mirror as he kisses her wet cheek. He licks the salty fluid from his lips. An evil grin fills his face. "All those warning signs, the little things that made you question me. More people should pay attention to that inner voice."

Chandra stares at a monster. She smells the leather as his fingers squeeze her neck. She squirms against him, struggling to breathe. His arm around her waist tightens. He lets go of her throat. She pants, sucking in air. Coughing erupts as the back of her throat burns.

"You should be happy to know they will find all kinds of evidence in Thomas' home. He will be convicted of your murder." Julian giggles. "At least I'm pretty sure he will. If not him, your neighbor Luke. He has been stalking you. He has a shit ton of pictures of you. So funny, too. In all my years doing this, I've never had this many people to blame for one murder."

"I can't believe I had feelings for you." Chandra's bottom lip quivers. "I can't believe how stupid I've been."

"You're not stupid. You're innocent. Naïve." Julian caresses her arms. His fingers brush against the side of her breast. "I'm pretty good at what I do. I've had a lot of practice. My one regret, I do wish I had just one night with you. One night to see your curves with no clothes on them. But I would've gotten too close. You've been one of my biggest distractions."

Chandra's body shakes. "I don't understand. You're a detective. A cop. Women, society, we trust you."

"Trust is overrated." He runs his hand through her hair. He wants to feel the silky strands against his fingers, but won't risk removing his gloves. Instead, he lifts a handful to his face. Letting them glide across his skin. His hand slides to her forehead. He bends her head back, exposing her neck. "You are a lovely creature." He kisses her cheek as he reaches behind his back. He pulls a knife from its sheathing. He drags the tip up her side. "I want you to know something." He watches her in the mirror. "Are you listening?"

She blinks, clearing the tears from her flooded eyes. Her lips roll together. Tears stream down her face. She squeaks as she nods.

"Don't worry. I'll take care of Theo. I've grown quite fond of him." In a quick flash he watches her eyes widen, as he slides the knife across her neck. He can hear gurgling as the blood gushes from the wound, spraying across the mirror.

Her eyes bulge as she watches her blood flow from her neck—her life draining from her. The last thing she sees is her own murder.

Her body goes limp in his arms. He steps back, letting her fall to the floor. A puddle of crimson oozes out around her.

Theo comes out from his hiding place and rubs against Julian's leg. He reaches down and picks up the cat. "Time to come to your new home." Julian steps around Chandra's lifeless body. Exiting the way he came in, he bundles Theo under his sweatshirt protecting him from the rain.

Chapter Thirty-Seven

Six months later

"Hi, mom."

"Hi, sweetie. Are you doing okay?"

"Things are going great. I'm looking over my schedule for my trip in a few weeks."

"I don't want you to go."

"Mom, I have to go. I'm scheduled to speak at several Tech events around the country." Theresa fills her glass with tea.

"I'm going to miss you that's all."

"Well, the good thing is I won't be leaving for three weeks. I'm kicking off the tour here in Manchester. I'm scheduled for several talks around here and Boston." Theresa adds sugar to her glass. She's standing at her kitchen window. Her house is one of the first ones on this street. Her yard backs up to a nature reserve. At least she will never have a back neighbor.

"I plan on being at the first one. I'm proud of you. What about the young man you have been seeing?"

"What about him?"

"I can't imagine your relationship will work if you're going to be traveling for weeks."

"Mom, we're more friends than anything serious. He helps with security at my company. We've been working together for a long time."

"Well, I like him."

"You like everyone."

"He is very handsome."

"Don't tell Julian that. His head will get too big." Theresa squints out the window. The sunset is casting crazy shadows across her lawn. She turns to grab a muffin from the fridge when she notices something toward the back by her trees. "What is that?"

"What is what, honey?"

"I don't know, Mom. I think I saw someone in my backyard."

Read on to enjoy a preview of <u>Innocence Taken. Book 1 in the Damien Kaine Series</u>.

Chapter 1

He straddled her chest—for leverage. His hands tingled as his fingers curled tight. He had to apply just the right amount of pressure. Her jerky movements increased as he squeezed her neck. The girl's chest hardened under his weight, holding on to the last bit of air in her lungs. The beautiful smoky brown color of her eyes faded, replaced with a dull gray cloud that crept from one side to the other. A gleeful smile tugged at his mouth when red dots popped on the sclera. Her bladder released, announcing the end. His fingers uncurled from her neck, and a heavy sigh escaped his lips. He stared down at her as the stillness and quiet of the room engulfed him.

The corners of his mouth twitched as his trip down memory lane was interrupted. He heard the begging from the far side of the room. He stared at the girl he held captive. He'd chosen this one because she resembled HER, but she didn't live up to his expectations. None did anymore. He wondered if he would ever find another like HER. The one thing all these girls had in common, they all begged— eventually. He turned away and finished the preparations.

• • • • ● • ● • • •

The thin mattress offered Becca little comfort. Leather straps bound her ankles and wrists to the bed. The slow melodic tune he whistled bounced off the cold concrete walls and pierced her eardrums like a hundred tiny pinpricks. Becca flinched at the sound of the chain hitting the floor as he hooked it to a ring in the ceiling. She closed her eyes. The man didn't care about her pleas. He had no plans to let her go.

She thought about how she got here. Becca's parents had given her a reprieve from her month-long grounding and allowed her to go to the mall with her two best friends. They chortled and bounced from store to store as they flirted with all the cute boys. The smell of freshly baked cookies and pretzels wafted through the air. Becca and her friends stopped for a snack and to chat with the boy behind the counter. That's where she met him, outside Cookie Crumbs. She bumped into him and then spent a few hours walking around the mall with him. Her stomach fluttered when he asked her to leave with him. What seemed like the best way to spend the remainder of her one day of freedom turned into the start of her worst nightmare.

Becca rocked back and forth muttering to herself. She watched him and prayed that he planned a quick death for her. As if he knew she stared at him, he glanced over his shoulder and winked at her. Becca shook uncontrollably, gasping for air as she clawed at the straps around her wrists.

Her eagerness to push her parents and their rules aside landed her here, in a cold, damp basement. Becca spent the last few months pushing as hard as she could to get away from her life. A life that seemed filled with endless chores and babysitting her little brother. As bad as she thought her life had been, these last few days were nothing short of Hell. She wanted that life back.

She cried out. "Oh God, please help me—please help me. Please, please help me." The sobs that choked her now burst out as her begging erupted into broken wails. The man turned and glowered at her, but she no longer cared. He planned to kill her. What did she care if he beat her before he did it? Becca leaned forward and wrapped her arms around her thighs. "I'm so sorry Mom, I'm so sorry." She hiccupped between the sobs. "I love you, Mom—Dad, I love you…" She repeated the mantra until her throat ached.

Becca saw the man turn and walk across the basement towards her. Her eyes widened; her prayers and pleas stopped. The man leered at her. She noticed the light as it bounced off the blade. Becca screamed.

Chapter 2

Division Central Chicago, IL

Lieutenant Damien Kaine dragged himself into the Vicious Crimes Unit. He plopped down at his desk, letting his arms hang limply. His athletic body sagged in his chair as he closed his eyes and leaned back. The air in the VCU hung thick and stale with the odor of burnt coffee and smelly socks. The stench made Damien's stomach roll. He blocked out the noise of the squad room and contemplated using his weapon on himself, the relief it might bring from the pounding in his head. Whiskey from the night before still coursed through his veins; flowing to the same beat that thumped inside his skull.

The morning had started off crappy when he threw his alarm clock against the wall. That made three this month. He could kick his own ass for letting Joe, his best friend and partner, talk him into going out last night. Damien had drunk too much, and today he paid the price. Hell, he'd been paying the price for several months now. Damien hadn't been a big drinker until the night he found Camilla in that hotel room. Since his canceled engagement, he and a bottle of whiskey spent a lot of time together.

He couldn't lay all the blame on Camilla, unfortunately. The job had taken its toll. The nightmares were never-ending. The dead never stayed dead. They liked to hang around in his dreams and bug the living shit out of him. Damien had considered turning in his resignation when Captain Mackey asked him to take the lieutenant's exam. Against his better judgment, he did. He passed. Now he felt stuck.

Damien opened one eye and checked his surroundings. VCU shared the seventh floor with the Electronics and Cyber Division. His eyes widened as he stared at the detectives behind the glass wall of the ECD enclosure. They never sat down. They danced and shimmied to an unheard rhythm. Damien imagined that beat came from the constant tapping of their fingers on computer keyboards. *Why do they move around so damn much?* His body shook at the disturbing sight.

Damien spun around in his chair. He ran a hand through his jet-black hair, causing it to stand in a wavy mess. Detective Jenkins sat across from him. Jenkins' shaggy brown hair hung over the collar of his shirt. It swayed a little every time he tossed that damn tennis ball into the air, which he did whenever he got stuck in a case. Usually, it didn't bother Damien, but today it added an echo to the thumping in his head. Jenkins was with them last night. He drank just as much as Damien did, and yet he looked like he hadn't touched one drop.

Detective Jenkins smiled at Damien who glowered back through bloodshot eyes. "Kaine, you sure don't seem as happy as you did last night at Mulligan's." Reclining in his chair, he stretched his long legs to the far side of his desk. "This morning you resemble dead dog shit warmed over. Nice hair—Lieutenant."

Damien pressed his lips tight to keep from smiling. "Fuck you, Jenkins."

"Ouch," Jenkins said. "Not very nice."

Detective Joe Hagan entered the VCU looking upbeat and well-rested. "Yo, Kaine, how do you feel this morning? Did we keep you out past your bedtime last night?"

Damien watched as Joe's muscular legs carried his linebacker body with the stealth of a panther, his dark red hair still wet from his morning shower. Damien hung his head in his hands. "You're a detective, you figure it out."

Joe's eyes narrowed as a broad grin pushed his cheeks up high. "Shit man, you're a wuss. A few drinks and you think you're going to die. Not to mention you're a cranky fucker, Lieutenant."

If Joe only knew it wasn't just a hangover from last night. There haven't been too many nights he hasn't used the bottle to help him sleep. Damien ransacked his desk looking for something to quiet the drum core in his head. "*Stai zitto!*" He snapped at Joe as he rubbed his temples.

"Yeah, yeah. Shut the hell up. Like I don't hear that every day." Joe reached into his desk drawer. "Hey cranky pants, here you go." Joe smiled as he threw a bottle at him.

Damien glanced up as the bottle smacked him in the chest. "Seriously you stupid fuck, can't you throw?"

Joe roared with laughter. "Can't you catch?"

"Whatever." Damien popped four aspirin into his mouth and washed them down with a gulp of the liquid this place tried to pass off as coffee. Hell, most of the time it didn't even resemble liquid. He peered into his coffee mug. "What the hell is this? It can't be coffee."

"Nope, it's Chicago Sludge," Joe said.

"Well, that explains why it smells and tastes like shit." Damien laid his head back against the chair. "How the hell can you be so fucking chipper? You drank more than I did."

"Aye, well, we Irish know how to hold our liquor. Plus, Melanie helped me sweat out any extra alcohol. You should've considered taking her friend home with you. I bet you'd be in a much better mood."

After he had called off his engagement, Damien decided there would be no more women. Well, no more relationships with women. A few one-night stands here or there was all Damien cared to indulge in. And he never spent the entire night with a woman—that meant some kind of commitment. Damien shook his head. "Who the hell is Melanie, and why the hell would I want to take her friend home?"

Joe sat on the corner of Damien's desk. "Melanie is a new waitress at Mulligan's. You would know this if you went out with me more often. Her friend wanted to make sure you got home okay and help tuck you into bed." Joe winked as he took a sip of his soda. "Anyway, turns out Melanie has quite the talent for sucking alcohol right out of your system. Her talents don't end there either. Did I mention she was a gymnast in high school? Damn, the positions that girl can get into, un-fucking-believable."

Detective Jenkins threw his head back and howled. "Dang, Joe. Have you slept with the entire female staff at Mulligan's?"

Joe smiled. "No, only a select few."

"Kaine, Hagan—you two in my office now!" The captain's booming voice reverberated off the walls.

Damien jolted upright. He rubbed his eyes hoping the Visine had worked. That morning, his dark blue eyes were almost indigo due to the red ring that surrounded them. He looked like a demon. Which seemed appropriate since he felt like he was in Hell anyway. His headache had receded, but his stomach churned and not because of the whiskey. As a former Marine and the director of VCU, Captain Mackey's anger could be a dangerous weapon. His six-foot four frame carried nothing but muscle, and his head held a lightning-fast brain.

Damien and Joe entered Mackey's office. The captain loomed behind a massive gunmetal gray desk he had brought with him to the VCU. His square face and wide, strong jaw rose above broad shoulders. Even sitting down, the captain commanded respect.

Damien scowled at Joe as he took a handful of jellybeans from the captain's candy jar.

Joe frowned at Damien. "What? He wouldn't have the damn jar if he didn't want us to eat them." Joe popped a handful of the colorful beans into his mouth.

Captain Mackey halfway snarled at Joe. "You might find yourself a few digits shy of a full hand one of these days Hagan."

Joe managed a sheepish grin as he sat.

Damien settled into a chair. His stomach had soured, and the knot that formed now tightened like a coil.

Captain Mackey clasped his hands together on his chest. "First, before we get started," he stared at Damien, "good job on passing the lieutenant's exam. Your ceremony will take place when you return. Starting immediately, you get the benefits of your rank, its privileges, and pay. We also need to discuss your new assignment."

Damien shifted in his seat searching for relief that wouldn't come from moving his ass around. His mouth tightened, and his face became taut and rigid. *When he returns? New assignment? What the hell did that mean?* He studied Mackey, looking for reassurances.

The captain's lip twitched. "Quit worrying, you're staying here, and you and Joe will remain partners." Captain Mackey shook his head. "Even though you two are my best detectives, you both are pains in my ass. Try to pay attention to what I'm about to say.

"I have been toying with the idea of putting a Lieutenant in charge of this Division. These bureaucratic fuckwads finally got their act together and put this damn Unit in place. When I first took this position as head of the VCU, I wanted to get this Unit set up and operating right.

"Now that the Unit is working the way it should, I have more responsibilities that need to be handled. Chief Rosenthal expects certain things from the captains here at Division Central, but as with any other government bureaucracy, shit always rolls downhill. I need someone who can take over the daily responsibilities of this Unit but who can also carry his own caseload.

"I need to put someone in place to handle this group and the Detectives in it. I want someone I can trust. That's you, Damien." Captain Mackey sat back and opened his desk drawer. "You'll report directly to me." Captain Mackey held a shield out for Damien. "Congratulations. You deserve this. You'd normally get your new shield at the ceremony, but since I must send you off on an assignment, I can't very well have you introduce yourself as a Lieutenant without a Lieutenant's shield."

Damien's mouth hung open as he stared at it. He never considered the possibility of being put in charge of the VCU. His hand shook when he reached for the shield with a sinking feeling in his gut—he wasn't sure if it was the whiskey remnants or that he didn't think he wanted the job.

The overhead light bounced off its shiny new surface. He ran his thumb across the front of the badge. Damien almost gave it back. It seemed to sizzle in his hand as if it knew he didn't deserve to hold it. His actions that night in the hotel should have put him behind bars.

He'd taken the exam thinking if he passed and made rank it would ignite his passion for the job again. He knew from early on he wanted to be a Homicide Detective. Damien felt responsible for helping these victims; they called out to him even in the silence of their death. What he saw daily made him question his own faith. Faith in God. Faith in the Catholic Church. Faith in his ability to uphold the very law he protected.

Damien glanced at Joe. One of the main things keeping him in this job, his friendship with Joe. He no longer knew if that was enough anymore. He forced a faint smile as he focused on the captain. "Wait, you're telling me I still have to be this knucklehead's partner?" He nodded towards Joe. "What happened to the perks of rank? This sounds more like punishment."

Joe punched him in the arm, the equivalent of a congratulatory hug. "Lieutenant or not, I'm the best damn partner you've ever had. Who else can put up with your Guinea ass?"

"Boys," Mackey growled. "You two are worse than my kids," he said as he pinched the bridge of his nose.

Damien started to say something smartass but saw that Captain Mackey's pleasant demeanor had changed. He opted to keep his mouth shut.

The captain sat up and placed his elbows on his desk. "A case has come in, and I want you guys to cover it." He opened the folder in front of him. "Locals who keep a strip of highway clean just outside Springfield, near Astoria, discovered the remains of a young girl."

Mackey's face flushed and his nostrils flared as he continued. "Crime Scene Techs have been dispatched, and they'll deliver everything collected to the Forensic Lab in Springfield. You two need to get down there. You'll work out of the lab. Director Jones will provide you with whatever you need. Kaine, you need to keep me updated on what you find every step of the investigation. Shoot me a daily report. I don't want any surprises on this. As of now, this hasn't been picked up by the media. Let's keep it that way if possible." He leaned back in his chair and raised an eyebrow. His gaze locked on Joe like a laser. "Stay out of trouble."

"What?" Joe shrugged. He grabbed another handful of jellybeans. "We never get in trouble, Captain."

"Sure you don't." Captain Mackey said. "Now go! Get the hell out of here." He waved them out the door.

· · · ● · ● · · · ·

"Fuck me running," Joe whispered. He hated cases like this. He had a younger sister, and these cases always hit a little too close to home.

Damien cocked his head towards Joe. "This day is just getting better."

Detective Jenkins stopped working on his computer as Damien and Joe walked back into the pen. "The expressions on your faces tell me that wasn't a friendly sit down with the captain."

Joe slammed his desk drawer shut. "Fucking—A on that. A cleanup crew discovered a murdered girl on the side of the road."

Jenkins winced. "Oh shit, where?"

"Outside Springfield," Joe said.

"What about Coach, Kaine? I mean Lieutenant." Jenkins asked with a wild grin. "You need someone to watch him?"

Damien clipped his new shield to his belt. "Jenkins, you hate cats. Why do you want to take care of mine? Wait, I know why—it's the only pussy you'll be able to get."

Jenkins' lips twitched. "Man, did that sense of humor come with your shiny new badge?"

Damien's smile filled his face as he tapped the shield. "Sure did. Maybe they'll put one of these in a Cracker Jack box because we all know that's the only way your sorry ass is gonna get one." Damien grabbed his jacket and nodded at Jenkins. "Thanks for your offer, Jenks. My neighbor Mrs. C. will watch after him. She takes him to her place and spoils him rotten. He loves it."

"Well, anytime you need me to take him I will," Jenkins said.

Damien shrugged. Coach showed up one day at his condominium and never left. With his rotund belly, Coach lorded over the condo as if it were his personal kingdom. Oddly enough, Coach had never liked Camilla.

Chapter 3

Damien threw his keys on the table near his front door and headed to the kitchen. He wanted to clean up his place before he packed and picked up Joe. He opened the fridge door, and within minutes, Coach strolled in. No matter where the cat hid in the condo when that refrigerator door opened, Coach magically appeared. Like a fat gargoyle, the cat perched himself next to Damien and beamed disappointment as he watched him clean it out.

"What?" He asked the cat as he scratched Coach's head. "I will be gone for a while, and this will stink by the time I come home. I'm damn sure your fat ass won't clean it out." *What the hell, I'm now talking to the cat like he can understand me.* Damien sighed. He scratched the cat's head. Coach head-butted Damien's thigh, then waddled back out on his beefy legs, no doubt in search of something soft and warm.

Forty minutes later, Damien finished cleaning and packing. He found Coach sprawled out on the sofa. The butterball opened one accusatory eye, questioning the interruption. "Mrs. C. will be by later to check on you. Try to lay off the kibbles, fat ass." Damien rubbed his belly and scratched under his chin. Coach stretched, yawned, and went back to sleep.

· · · · ● · ● · · · ·

Joe had finished packing his bags and sat in the quiet of his large apartment, glancing around. On the top floor of a two-family home, the high ceilings gave it an open and airy feeling. The couple who owned the house lived on the first floor and traveled extensively. In the summer he enjoyed the back deck. It overlooked a park and a wooded area. He had furnished the space with oversized furniture that invited visitors to stay awhile. He'd dated this interior designer for a few months, and she tired of his bachelor pad décor and decorated it for him.

Joe smiled at the memory. The woman's talents didn't just stop at interior decorating. She had a very adventurous streak in bed. *Damn, I should call her when I get back*. He frowned. Joe remembered why he'd quit seeing her—she assumed that because they were intimate, they were on the verge of getting married. He'd come close to that once with a horrible ending. *Yeah, not gonna happen.* Plus, he had witnessed firsthand all the crap Damien had gone through with Camilla, no way. Joe didn't want that kind of relationship. Not for a long time. If ever. He wasn't the settling down type. He enjoyed dating a variety of women.

Joe looked at his watch. He leaned back in his chair closing his eyes. He tried to shove everything out of his mind, just relax and enjoy the silence. But he couldn't. His thoughts circled back to Damien.

Over the past few months, he'd watched his friend and partner transform into a different person. Ever since he broke it off with Camilla. Truth be known, Joe couldn't stand her. Joe knew from the start Damien shouldn't have been with her, but he kept his mouth shut. His friend had to figure it out on his own.

Damien never explained what caused their break up, and Joe never pressed for information. He figured Damien would tell him when he felt ready. Now with this case and a three-hour ride ahead of them, Joe might broach the subject. He knew his friend well enough to know a break up wouldn't make him act this way. There had to be something else.

Joe jumped at the sound of Damien's horn. "Showtime," he said with one last look around his place. Joe bounded down the stairs and heaved his two bags into the back of the SUV, climbed into the passenger seat, and moved it back as far as he could.

Joe stretched out his long legs. "You ready for this?"

"No, but what choice do we have?"

A broad grin formed across Joe's face. "How's your headache?"

Damien smirked. "Ha ha. You're such a friggin hoot. I doubt you'd have been laughing if my head had exploded and you'd had to clean my brain matter off the walls of VCU."

Van Halen's *Jump* rang out from Damien's phone. The dash's video screen displayed a phone number of a person he had no desire to speak with, especially with Joe sitting right next to him. "Oh crap, just take my gun and shoot me." Damien dragged his hand through his hair pulling on the ends. "Yeah, Kaine here."

"Hey baby, how're you doing?"

"Camilla, I'm not your fucking baby. Why the hell do you keep calling me?"

"I wanted to know how things are going and see if you wanted to get together this week."

Her raspy voice used to sound sexy to him. Now, it made Damien want to jab a stick in his ear. Damien clenched his jaw. "Camilla, I told you, I don't want to see you again, ever. What part of that conversation did you not understand?"

"Come on Damien, I miss you. I want another chance. I'm sorry. You know I love you. Please, let's get together and talk."

Damien smacked his hand against the steering wheel. "You have a problem understanding me. I do not want to see or speak to you at all! *Capisci*?"

"Please Damien, I made a mistake. How long are you going to hold it against me? Things snowballed, and I did things I shouldn't have done. Please, give me—give us another chance."

"Are you fucking kidding me? A mistake? You call banging some suit in your office, repeatedly, a mistake? You're fucking delusional. It's been over for almost a year. It will stay that way. Hell, it had been over long before I threw your crap out of the condo. You screwed up Camilla! Now you can live with the fucking consequences!"

"Pleeease Damien, I'm sor–"

Damien disconnected the call. "Well, shit, shit, shit! What a fucking miserable day."

Joe's eyes bulged, and his jaw hung to his lap. "You didn't tell me she cheated on you."

"No, I didn't," Damien said with a little more venom than he intended. "I told no one except my dad, and that was hard enough. She cheated several times and lied about all sorts of shit. I wanted her out of my life." Damien glanced over at Joe. "I wanted no one, you included, telling me 'I told you so.'"

Joe scowled. "Hey, I might have said she wasn't the right girl for you, but I never would have rubbed it in your face. Especially if I had known, she cheated on you. As your Italian tongue would say, she's a *stupida cagna*, and you deserve so much better."

Damien ran his hand over his face. "Yeah, she is a stupid bitch. So, now you know." He turned and stared out the window. He looked back at Joe, "Man, it never occurred to me she would do something like that. I gave her everything she wanted. Treated her like a damn queen. I loved her. Loved her more than I thought I could ever love a woman." Damien had told no one about how he found out Camilla was cheating on him, with who, or what had happened that night in the hotel room.

Joe punched him on the shoulder. "Better it happened now rather than after you'd married her." He grinned at Damien. "Next time save yourself the hassle and listen to what I say. You know I always watch out for you."

He gave Joe an easy smile. "Yeah, next time I will." The knot in Damien's stomach tightened just a little more. Joe had proven himself a damn good friend and partner, and he deserved to know the whole truth.

Joe pulled out his notepad. "So, about this case, Astoria is a small community with roughly a couple thousand in population. Seems like nothing but farm country in that area. The stretch of Highway 24 where they discovered the girl has nothing but pastures surrounding it. No buildings, no houses, no nothing. I'm leaning towards dumpsite only."

Damien took a swig of soda. He glanced at the can. Joe had gotten him hooked on this diet soda. Everyone at Central gave them hell for it too. "Since the CST's will be back at the lab before we get to town, I say we go there first. We can hit the dumpsite later if we need to."

Joe patted his stomach. "Sounds good. Now swing through someplace and let's get some food."

"You're always hungry. Didn't you eat breakfast like two hours ago?"

"Sure, key phrase—hours ago. I took an enormous dump at the house before you got there. Now I'm hungry again."

"Seriously, dude why do you tell me these things? I don't need to know about your bowel movements. You know you're going to end up being a *vacca grassa*—fat cow—if you don't watch it." Damien chuckled as Joe gave him the finger.

Chapter 4

He sat and watched her apartment. Waiting. He looked at his watch, anytime now, he thought. He had first seen her a few weeks back, at the outdoor market he sometimes delivered to. He couldn't believe it when he saw her either. She looked like she could pass as HER older sister. Her short and very curvy build was a little different than what he normally went for. God, she was beautiful, though. He had been so close to her in the parking lot, just a few feet away. He almost grabbed her then, but the timing wasn't right. However, he followed her home that day. Knowing where she lived had allowed him to follow her regularly.

He saw her again at the mall, the day he took Becca. He bumped into her and couldn't believe it was her. He'd considered pursuing her, but it had been too hard to approach her. He didn't think she would fall for the same lines he used on the others. After all, she wasn't as young as they were. He'd come close to following and taking her that day, but then he saw Becca. More his type and much easier prey.

His phone rang. "Yeah, what's wrong now?" He barked into the phone. "Well, what the hell am I paying you for? How the hell should I know? They're fucking farm animals." He laughed. "No shit. You're right about that. They are only good for cooking. Get over there and get them. Tell the old man we keep trying to keep them from getting out. I don't think he's too pissed. He has never complained formally. I'm about an hour from home. I should be there soon." He threw his phone in the passenger seat.

He reached for the ignition about to start his truck when she came out. He had a direct line of sight to her. She locked her door and headed down the walkway. She always parked in front of her apartment.

He watched as she threw her bags into her car. She wore a pink shirt and her dark brown hair contrasted nicely against it. For a moment, she paused at the driver's side before she got in. His heart raced as she looked in his direction. He sunk in his seat. He was sure she couldn't see him, but what if she did? She might remember him. He cursed himself. This was a stupid idea. He didn't do stupid. He hated stupid. But God, he wanted her.

She got into her car and drove off. He almost thought about following her, but he had to get back to the farm. That's okay, he thought. He knew where she liked to go and knew where she lived. He knew where she worked too, but that didn't scare him. He would just make sure he took her far away from her office.

Chapter 5

Forensic Lab

The Springfield Forensic Laboratory was comprised of several buildings connected by a series of underground tunnels; making it easy for employees to travel between the buildings on the large compound. Damien drove down the winding drive to the main building, which housed DNA, Trace, Autopsy, and the Administrative offices.

A stunning brunette greeted them at the front desk. Joe gave Damien a sly smile and sauntered over to her. She wore a name tag centered above one perfectly shaped breast. He leaned in close to her and lowered his voice. "Hey, there—Taylor Reese. I'm Detective Joe Hagan and this," he nodded towards his right, "is Lieutenant Damien Kaine. We're from Division Central. We need to speak with Director Jones. Is he available?" Joe smiled one of his sexiest smiles at her.

"Sure, let me call back there. One moment please." Her shaky finger punched a few numbers on the keypad. "Jamie, the two Detectives from Chicago are here to meet with the director. No, they're standing right here. Okay, I'll let them know. What? Oh yeah, no I don't know who he is. I've seen him at that track by the outdoor mall I go to. No. First I will ask Matt to look into it. Yes. I will tell the director if it keeps happening. Okay, I will. Thanks, Jamie." Taylor smiled at Joe. She could feel her cheeks burn as she stared at him. "The director will be with you in a moment," she said.

Damien and Joe stepped away from the desk. Damien hung his head to hide his smile. "Dude quit gawking at her. Can't you see you're making her nervous?"

Joe frowned at Damien. "I'm not making her nervous," Joe said.

Damien chuckled. "Right. She can't even make eye contact with you. Look at yourself, you're drooling right now. Just remember why we are here, Casanova. You need to keep your head on straight."

A wicked grin spread across Joe's face. "Jealous, huh?"

"Yeah, you got me. I'm jealous."

• • • • • • • • • • •

"Lieutenant Kaine and Detective Hagan," Director Jones said as he walked towards them. He shook both of their hands and guided them to the doors he had come through. Sliding a key card through the security lock, the light on the keypad flashed green.

Director Jones pushed open the heavy metal doors and led them down a corridor. "I spoke with Captain Mackey, not ten minutes ago. I'm glad to have you two here."

Damien liked the director right off. He had a lean body carried by legs with a long smooth stride. He looked as if he glided down the hallway with minimum effort. Unlike Captain Mackey, Director Jones wore his authority casually. Damien had no doubt that the director's casual demeanor left no room for his authority to be questioned, under any circumstances.

Director Jones stopped in front of an empty room. "As you can see, we set up a whiteboard and two laptops for you. If you find you need anything else, let me know or ask Taylor up front. She always knows how to reach me. Have you checked into a hotel yet?" Jones continued down the hallway.

"No. Not yet," Damien said. "We passed a couple on our way. We figured we'd get one of those after we finished up here."

"Don't worry about the arrangements. I'll tell Taylor to get you two rooms at the Holiday Inn down the street. That way you can stay here as long as you need to."

"Sounds good. Thanks," Damien said. "What do we have?"

"The CSTs got back about an hour ago. The ME is already in autopsy with the body. We're checking her fingerprints now. We're also tracking down some missing person reports. The girl seems about seventeen or eighteen. The killer didn't cut her face, but it has some hellacious bruising."

As they reached another set of metal doors, Director Jones stopped and hung his head. "I've seen some pretty nasty crap in my day, but this—it's one of the worst. He cut her into pieces and then put her body parts in a heavy-duty plastic bag."

Director Jones used his keycard to unlock the door. A hiss escaped as the door swung open. The heavy scent of disinfectant wafted out. Classic soul music emanated from a room at the end of the corridor. They walked down the long dimly lit hallway. With every two or three steps, an overhead fluorescent bulb clicked on, creating eerie shadows on the walls. Damien sensed those shadows were the dead that traveled through these doors.

"This is Dr. Langley, our Medical Examiner," Jones said.

Damien stepped forward. Doctor Langley's blond hair glistened under the glare of the lights. A bright blue lab coat draped his broad shoulders. He had to be in his fifties with the body of a much younger man.

Hunched over a steel slab, Doctor Langley smiled at the two Detectives. "Music off. Sorry, I play my music a little too loud. Detectives, pleased to meet you. I wish we were meeting under better circumstances." His gaze shifted to the table in front of him.

"Same here Doc. Do you have anything yet?" Damien asked, moving up to the table. All the air in his lungs hissed out.

Joe followed Damien and took two steps closer to the table. "Fucking bloody hell!" His Irish lilt heavier than usual.

The remains of a once beautiful young girl lay before them. The girl's hair, a matted mess of tangles and dried blood. Her head clung to her torso by a few tethers of tendons, ligaments, and skin. It laid on its side, and her dull cloudy eyes glared at Damien and Joe. Her head couldn't even rest in the U-shaped headrest most of the dead had the privilege of using.

Dr. Langley rested a hand on the top of the girl's head with the tenderness a loving father might do as he watched his daughter sleep. "Well, as you can see, we're having trouble stabilizing her head. The killer cut her arms off at the shoulders and then separated them at the elbows. He then removed her legs at the thighs and separated them at the knees."

The ME exhaled a long heavy breath. "Upon preliminary findings, it appears she suffered repeated sexual assaults, both vaginal and anal. The tearing indicates severe trauma. From the destruction of the tissue, I would say he used some kind of instrument at some point."

Joe dragged his hand down his face. "Damn."

Damien stared down at the young girl. Above one of her breasts, there appeared to be a deep indentation. "Doctor Langley, are those bite marks on her chest?"

The Doctor glanced up at Damien's stoic face. "Yes, Lieutenant. There are several bite marks on her breasts and her shoulder area. We will cast those for future identification of our suspect. Bite marks are as individual as fingerprints. They can be tricky to cast, but when done properly it will stand up in court. However, something that isn't tricky to do is figure out what she ate last." Dr. Langley held a small container filled with a cloudy liquid. "Once I analyze this, her stomach contents—or lack thereof. It seems he gave her limited food and fluids while he held her."

Dr. Langley rolled his shoulders and twisted his head from side to side, causing Joe to wince at the cracking sound. "We took samples for DNA. We could get a hit if her parents put her in the system. Last year during Abduction Awareness Week, we made DNA/Fingerprint kits available to every school-age child's parents. We had widespread participation in the program. There is a good chance we can identify her quickly."

Damien clutched the St. Michael medal he wore around his neck. His chest constricted. The trauma this innocent girl suffered sickened him. He swallowed the lump in his throat and pushed down the bile trying to work its way out.

· · · · ● · · ● · · · ·

Just outside the conference room door, Damien stood with Joe and the director. Jones' jaw clenched. "One hell of a way to start the week. I want this bastard. I have a fourteen-year-old daughter. This hits too close to home."

Damien spun around at the sound of footsteps jogging towards them. A young man who looked barely twenty-one came down the hall. "Sir, we have the identity of the young girl. Rebecca 'Becca' Martin through her fingerprints. The parents registered both their kids last year with those DNA/Fingerprint kits. She went missing from a mall in Decatur last Saturday afternoon. Her family lives in Blue Mound, thirty-five miles up Interstate 72."

Jones nodded. "Good job Matt. Let DNA know she's in the system." Jones glanced at Joe and Damien. "We placed those cards and samples in a different catalog for easy indexing. When we have a missing child, time is of the essence." Jones watched the young man as he headed back to his work area. "Well, I don't envy your next stop, family notifications suck." He handed them several of his business cards. "You met Matt Dillard, one of our lab techs. He'll assist you here in the lab. If you need him to gather information on the computer or get anything for you, just contact him."

Director Jones handed one of Matt's cards to Damien. "You two, don't forget to get your ID badges at the desk. It'll allow you twenty-four-hour access to the lab while you're here. Give me your cards; I'll pass them on to Matt." He took the cards from Damien and Joe and headed down the hallway.

Damien studied his watch as if it gave him instructions. "It's now four p.m. What do you say we go over to the hotel, drop our stuff off and then head up to Blue Mound? I could use a few minutes before we tell the parents about their daughter. Let's also call the local Sheriff's office and make sure we can stop by and speak with him before we head out to the parent's house. I'm hoping he has something that will help us in this case."

"Sounds good. I wouldn't mind a few minutes to clear my head, and maybe throw up my lunch." Joe said.

To read more of <u>Innocence Taken, download the Ebook</u> from your favorite retailer.

Damien Kaine Thrillers

Derek Reed Thrillers

Novellas

Short Stories

Find them all at her website:

www.whiskeyandwriting.com

Victoria M. Patton lives with her husband of twenty-five years, two dogs—Bogart and Georgie, and two cats—Squeakers and Pumpkin.

Her years in the Coast Guard doing Search and Rescue/Law Enforcement and her BS in Forensic Chemistry helps her figure out the best way to hide all the bodies, and then write thrilling stories to keep you up at night. If she has any free time, she drinks copious amounts of whiskey and binge watches Hulu and Acorn TV.

Check out her blog Whiskey and Writing where she tries to help new authors navigate the indie publishing world. If all else fails, she provides great whiskey recipes.

Email her at: **victoria@victoriampatton.com**.

Check out her author website at www.victoriampatton.com. Be sure to join her Email List for updates on her latest book.

Follow her at Facebook @WhsikeyandWriting Twitter @victoriampatton and on Pinterest @victoriampatton.